HARD
CASH

Get the Water Street Crime Starter Library
FOR FREE

Sign up for the no-spam newsletter and get *four* full-length ebooks—the thrillers ***BLOODY PARADISE***, ***FROM ICE TO ASHES***, ***TROPICAL ICE***, and ***SING FOR THE DEAD***—plus two introductory short stories by the author of ***STAINED FORTUNE***, ***MONEY FAUCET*** and ***HARD CASH*** and lots more exclusive content, all for *free*.

Details can be found at the end of *HARD CASH*, or go here now: mailchi.mp/waterstreetpressbooks.com/ waterstreetcrimemailinglist

HARD CASH

JOE CALDERWOOD

Water Street Press
Healdsburg, California

Published by Water Street Press
Healdsburg, California

Water Street Press paperback edition published 2019

Produced in the USA

Print 978-1-62134-422-3
E-Pub 978-1-62134-423-0
Mobi 978-1-62134-424-7

Cover design by **thecovercollection.com**

Typesetting services by **bookow.com**

Dedicated to my spouse, Gil, for thirty-nine years of excitement and putting up with my obsessions.

Acknowledgments

I want to thank my editor, Lynn Vannucci, for sorting through all my writings to make sense out of my story.

Chapter 1

Don't let anyone kid you: crime *does* pay.

At least, that was my take on life in early November 2009.

Pablo and I flew into El Lencero Airport for the funeral on my Gulfstream, not his, because my toy was new and I wanted another opportunity to fly through the skies—even if only from Mérida to Sonora—on my own wings.

He and I wore bespoke suits for the occasion —mine of the most delicate, charcoal-black baby alpaca wool from Hungary, from the hand of the house of Boglioli, and Pablo's of the finest cream-colored Irish linen available to his own Italian tailor, Mr. Massimo Piombo. And we sipped a bottle of Bollinger Les Vieilles Vignes Francaises—from mouth-blown Zalto Denk'Art flutes—as we flew.

Six bodyguards traveled with us—Pablo's, not mine; even given my line of work and all the intrigue it had recently fostered, it had not occurred to me that I might want my own security detail. The men, all in dapper black, shoulder holsters causing not even one errant bulge beneath their sleek-fitting suits, rode at the front of the plane, studiously separated from Pablo and me at the back, yet utterly silent, attuned to the conversation between us and a mere raised finger away from intervening, should— I don't know. Should I suddenly sit up in my seat and raise my voice to their boss? Wag a finger at him? Punch the elegant Pablo in the nose? Even if that was my style, I'm smart enough not to fuck with a bunch of guys who look like they could be extras in a Francis Ford Coppola movie.

"It is not customary to wear white to funerals, in my country," I offered, stretching my shoulders and slouching deeper into the leather of the seat I occupied.

"Nor in mine," Pablo conceded, and then he shrugged. "But what am I to do? I am most comfortable in white linen—it is my signature, you know? If someone does not want me to wear white linen to his funeral, then he should not die."

I chuckled because, really, what else was I supposed to do? Of the dozen—or so—drug lords for whom I laundered money, Pablo Navarro was the emperor, the undisputed leader of the pack. I'd worked for his pack, under his aegis, for just over a year at that point, putting an average of eight million dollars a day through my wringer in Mexico and making it come out all sparkling white and fluff-dried on the other side: in America; the bank I owned in Miami. I took my five percent right off the top and kept my head down, asking no questions and telling no lies. Still, these funerals—all to lay to rest Pablo's fellow lords who'd been taken out in what Pablo described as a "housecleaning", three of them in the course of just five days—gave me pause. I was still unsure what part, if any, Pablo had played in their demise.

I was not looking forward to the funeral, certainly. The first two had been dull, droning affairs involving High Masses and plenty of incense, and I knew what I was in for as we winged our way to Sonora. I had grown up in Southern Florida in the '90s, in many ways a typical American kid, unpracticed in the Protestant faith with which my mother was titularly affiliated, and the rites and rituals of the Catholic lords had intrigued me, at the start; by the third funeral they had lost their mystery. I found the service tedious, the priests long-winded, and the wailing of the widows and other women, shadowed in their black veils, absolutely heartbreaking.

At the first funeral, Emiliano's, in his territory, Mexicali, the week before, I hadn't had the luxury of being bored. I'd just returned to Mexico from a week's enforced vacation in Miami, where Pablo had insisted I lay low while the housecleaning had been in progress, and I was not especially comforted by the idea that Pablo had kept me away for my own good. Sure, he wanted me out of the way while the ranks of his Mexican brethren were being summarily reduced—with or without his direction; again, at this point I hadn't a clue about that—but what was going to happen to me when the housecleaning was complete and I returned to my home in Mérida? Killing me on Mexican soil would be so much more convenient for Pablo, where he had a veritable army of men at his command and the law was disposed to look the other way when he acted out. In spite of the fact that Pablo himself had welcomed me back to Mexico with open arms, I had been on my toes while we laid Emiliano to rest—and only slightly distracted by the intricacies of the Catholic funeral service, watching Pablo to take my cues from him about when to stand, when to sit, when to kneel.

By the time of the second funeral—Felipe's in Matamoros, four days ago—I had moved from a state of constant red alert to a more manageable phase of paranoia: was I still of use to Pablo? I had always understood, on an intellectual level, that the friendship he and I sustained was based on mutual need: he needed me to turn his money into currency he could easily access, and I needed —or, well, at least greatly *desired*—the income I made doing my part of his dirty work. I knew that finding another American banker to take him on as a client would be difficult, though not impossible—it was 2009 when we began our relationship, after all, and a lot of banks, not just mine, were scrambling to stay afloat after the American economic bubble burst. I wondered if Tim, my assistant, had been too efficient about doing the work I delegated to him—running the armored cars to and from Mérida to cartel HQs all over Mexico to collect drug industry profits, and sitting at the elbow of my Mexican banker, Juan Carlos at Reforma Bank, while the day's transfers were processed; perhaps I'd not been hands-on as much as I should have been, delegated thoughtlessly, and now Pablo had come to the conclusion that paying me five percent was wasteful spending. Had he concluded that it would be more profitable for him to simply hire Tim to do the work for a drastically cut rate? I had, however, by the time of Filipe's funeral, some sense that if Pablo wanted me dead and out of the way, it would have happened already. Still, I was in no way comfortable with what the future might hold.

This, the third funeral, the final one, so far as I knew—Matias's in Sonora—found me more willing to relax about my place, and its continuance, in Pablo's organization. I'd been back in Mexico for six full days by this point, and Pablo had invited me for dinner several times—to his vineyard in Guadalajara, to his hacienda near Mérida, and, once, to Kuuk, a favorite restaurant in Mérida where we indulged in the out-of-this-world tasting menu and enough wine that Pablo had dismissed his car and allowed me to drive him (and, of course, two of his bodyguards) back to my place for a nightcap and a dip in my pool. We'd genuinely had a great time together that night; I did not think Pablo was that good of an actor.

Also, I was growing comfortable with my familiarity with the Catholic services. I no longer needed to glance out of the corner of my eye to know when to stand or kneel, and I could sing some of the lyrics, in Spanish, to the more popular funeral hymns. I also knew enough not to try to enter the church immediately upon arrival but to wait outside for the Reception of the Body.

As the congregation recessed from Matias's service at the Catedral de la Ascunsion, the jewel of the forty-nine parishes within the Archdiocese of Hermosillo, Pablo clapped me on the back, commanded, "Come," and steered me away from the steps of the wondrous building, toward where two of his men stood by one of the two shiny, dark-blue Lincoln Town Cars that had been reserved for his use while he was in Sonora. I did so willingly but, as I seated myself, noticed that the driver of our blue Lincoln was not jostling for a place in the funeral procession. He was following the lead Town Car, making a tight left turn away from the cluster of cars at the front of the church, to go in the opposite direction.

This was unusual. After the other funerals we'd gone to the grave sites, then on to the homes of the widows to partake in a feast of outstanding local food and shared memories of the deceased. We'd never stayed at these after-parties, so to speak, for very long, but we put in a showing; that we were clearly going to be skipping this part of the occasion in Sonora put me more closely to the edge than I'd been all week long. Adrenaline poured into my bloodstream as if it came bottled in a gallon jug, glugging into my system in thick, powerful bursts.

Pablo, who'd taken the seat beside me in the back of the car, clamped his hand on my thigh and squeezed just above my knee until it was almost painful. "I've had my fill of grieving," he said, looking ahead, around, at the two men who rode with us or out the windows, but not at me. "I would rather, this afternoon, to have steak." I closed my eyes against the agony Pablo was causing my knee and tried not to wince. "After all, we are in the meat capital of all Mexico!" Pablo might have been thirty years older than I was, but his hands were strong. Like a vise grip on my trembling thigh. "Sonora! Even the word makes you crave beef, no?" he asked and released his hold on my leg.

I managed to take a deep breath, as if sucking in the whole of my thirty-some years on the planet, wondering if I really was going to die so young. Then I felt the hard swat of Pablo's palm on my throbbing thigh. "Yes! Take another deep breath, Clint—you can almost smell the slaughterhouses!"

Chapter 2

To my great relief, the blue Lincoln took us to Villa de Seris, Restaurant Palominos, and actual beef—two extraordinary, rare *filete supremos*. The cabernet Pablo had ordered to go with our beef was, I noted as he poured, from California—Silver Oak; between us, Pablo was the oenophile, and quite dedicated to growing, bottling, and promoting Mexican wines, so I declined to comment on his choice. Pablo tasted his steak, sipped his wine, declared that both were "*Excelente*!" and, turning to the window we were seated before, gave a little salute to his men who waited outside. "Rafael," he called, gesturing to our waiter with his knife and ordering steaks to be sent to his security detail.

We tucked into our food then and, still fighting the trace adrenaline making my heart beat double time, I let Pablo take the lead in our conversation. Clearly, he had something he wanted to say to me. "Well, now we have buried three of our own..." was how he chose to begin.

I looked at the steak bleeding on my plate. "Not *our* own, I think," I replied. But softly.

Pablo chewed, swallowed, drank, returned his glass to its place on the table, put his fork on his plate, and lifted his napkin from his lap to his lips. Only when he'd wiped away a drop of cabernet from the corner of his mouth did he smile. "I know that you have been wondering what's happening here in Mexico while you were away," he said, "and I think I would like to tell you."

I nodded, grateful that I had a mouthful of steak and couldn't speak.

Pablo lifted his wine again and sat back in his chair. "From time to time, every business must reassess its operations, steer itself back to its core strengths."

I frowned. I was used to Pablo talking in metaphors and euphemisms, but I was not used to him talking like an MBA candidate. I took my time chewing.

"Our departed fellows in these border towns," Pablo continued, waving a hand to indicate geography, "they were not content with the profits they enjoyed from our core business. They wanted to expand their interests, into areas where they have no expertise—and for which we have little taste."

I looked up and caught Pablo's eye. "We?" I asked.

"Me. *I* have little taste for human trafficking, Clint. Our pathways into the US gave these men some notion they would be able to transport people as well as our more customary wares, and I do not like this."

I didn't immediately think adding 'coyote' to the drug runners' job descriptions was a completely unreasonable business decision. I, too, had interests beyond the work I did for Pablo and his cohorts, and none of them got in the way of my taking good care of his business. "If they could help to safely get people to a better life, a life that the people themselves desire, why not?"

Pablo had picked up his utensils again, in preparation to cut another piece of steak, but instead of targeting the beef on his plate he pointed the knife at me. "One hundred thousand pesos at the start! This is what they were asking! *Ladrones*! Before they would even let the people stuff themselves into their boat or their truck or their tunnel, they asked for one hundred thousand pesos, and on the other side, they said to the people, 'Oh, you think you have paid for this trip? No, no!' and demanded one hundred thousand more! If the people or their families did not or could not pay, they held them for ransom. Kept them imprisoned in the hull of a boat or a metal shed on a *bastardo* rancher's land just over the border from this very town. They gave them no food, no water, no relief and, if they died in captivity? Well, this is the cost of doing business! Many innocents died for their greed!"

At this point Pablo put down his knife and shoved a huge bite of steak into his mouth. He chewed it as if it were a meditative exercise, slowly calming himself.

Then he continued: "You do not kill honest men who want only honest work for honest pay. You do not make women and children miserable for your profit. You do not swindle your countrymen!"

Here he took a large swallow of wine.

"I told them not to do this, and yet this is what they did. It was necessary to demonstrate my objection in the clearest way possible."

He took another long drink.

"I think that I have made my point to the ones that remain. They will not so easily ignore my advice from now on." He nodded, as if approving of what he'd just said—of how he'd handled the problem—and picked up his knife and fork for another bite of bloody beef.

I took a moment, trying to think of an appropriate response. Pablo possessed a fortress—a virtually impenetrable underground bunker on the south side of the Gulf of Mexico, in the small pueblo Chuburna, far away from the hectic pace of his headquarters in Mérida. He'd built it beneath an ancient stone temple, at the end of a scarred and rutted road, deep in the rain forest. It was there Pablo maintained an armory that put the munitions available to the entire Mexican military to shame, knowing that the government would never destroy the temple, it being such an integral piece of the nation's heritage. It was there that a security and surveillance operation to rival NASA's was centered. It was there, a hundred feet below the earth, encased in lead and powered by his own, personal solar field, that Pablo kept a subterranean mansion furnished in French antiques and a library of first editions, all set amid rose marble floors and pillars. This bunker was where the drug lords gathered, in the lap of luxury and Pablo's exquisite taste, when there was business to discuss—it was, in fact, where I'd been taken the year before to meet the heads of the cartels so I could pitch my money-laundering scheme to them. I wondered that Pablo hadn't called the lords together in this place to hash out their entry into the field of human trafficking. Lay down a few ground rules to make the operation humane. Set some standard fee for the service— a more affordable fee, if Pablo was so inclined.

When I'd met the group of them, Pablo's colleagues had seemed like such refined men—nothing as I'd imagined a bunch of Mexican drug lords would be—and there had seemed to be such amity among them. Surely, they could have worked together to decide on terms that would have been agreeable to all of them. Business was business, and these were businessmen, interested above all in profitability; they sold drugs for a living, after all.

Before I could put all these thoughts in order and work out a way to express them to Pablo without further agitating him, a shot rang out. I heard it a nanosecond before the window we were sitting in front of shattered, sending shards of tempered glass flying onto our plates and into our hair.

There was no time to be stunned as this first shot was followed by a barrage of more shots, gunfire like fireworks. Still, I had enough presence of mind to dive to the floor, under the table where Pablo had already taken cover. I skidded on my way down, my Ferragamos leaving a streak of blood on the terrazzo floor. It flashed through my mind that the blood was from the steaks and, just as instantaneously, I realized that only a naïf could entertain denial like that. I started patting myself, looking for a wound, thinking that, even though there was blood, I couldn't be wounded because I felt no pain, though that could be shock—

"It's me," Pablo grunted.

I turned to where he was sprawled beneath the tablecloth. He was bleeding from his shoulder, a stain of red spreading on the pristine white of his linen suit. "Oh, Jesus," I breathed. On instinct, because the bullets were still flying above us and there was no room in my adrenaline-fired brain for rational thought, I reached from under the table to grab the napkin that had fallen from my lap when I'd dived, ripped Pablo's jacket open and pressed it hard into the gaping hole just under his collar bone.

There was so much blood. The only other time I'd seen a quantity of blood like this was the evening I'd walked into my guest room in Pablo's bunker and found one of the drug lords—the beautiful maniac, Alvaro—beheaded in my bed. I rethought my observation about the fellowship among the thieves who were my colleagues; had Alvaro been the outlier I'd assumed, too dangerous to be allowed to live even among criminals? Deserving of his demise? His death a relief, even if I'd have preferred it hadn't been accomplished on *my* feather bed? But who among the lords would mark *Pablo* for assassination?

The napkin was sopping with Pablo's blood almost as soon as I pressed it to his wound, my shaking hands drenched in red. Pablo must have noticed my own blood had drained from my face. My quivering lips and hands. "Flesh wound," he assured me, grunting through gritted teeth. "Hurts like a son of a bitch though—"

Chapter 3

RAFAEL, our waiter, and two men whose crisp white jackets identified them as part of Restaurant Palominos' kitchen staff, pulled Pablo out from under the table quickly but with great care, and jostled me from beneath the tablecloth with considerably less gentleness.

When had the gunfire stopped? *Had* it stopped? I would have been happy enough to stay huddled on the terrazzo floor for the rest of my life if that's what it took until I was sure the *rat-tat-tat* of automatic weapons was just an echo in my head and not the result of enemies outside the restaurant mowing down anyone who popped his head up, vermin in some sick whack-a-mole game.

Not that I'm a coward. Risk is my modus operandi, adrenaline my drug of choice. It's just that I prefer my risks to involve the thrill of executing a financially-savvy end-run around the ATF, not outrunning half a dozen AK-47s. Rafael, however, was insistent. "Come on, mister," he prodded me, yanking on my arm until I made it to my feet and, following his example, hunched from the waist, we hustled to the back of the restaurant and through the kitchen's double doors.

"Three of them, boss." One of Pablo's men—the imposing Enio, six-three, two-eighty, shiny bald—was standing over the emperor who lay flat on his back on the greasy black mats in front of the hot window. The crisp white jackets of the two sous chefs who'd dragged Pablo out of harm's way were spattered with red. They knelt, one at his head and one at his feet, one exchanging my drenched napkin with a fresh one to Pablo's wound and the other loosening the pants at Pablo's waist in an effort to help his labored breathing.

"Three shooters?" Pablo asked between gasps for air.

Enio blinked. Don't ever let anyone tell you that professional thugs don't blink. Or that they don't break a sweat. Enio mopped his face and head with the kitchen towel Rafael handed him and opened his eyes before he spoke. "Three of ours, boss. Three of them dead."

Pablo groaned. Not from the pain.

"We don't know how many shooters—they fired from a van and it was in and out too fast to know. Shooters, we think, maybe three or four. At least."

Pablo nodded. Conserving his energy.

I was as useless as I felt. It might have been less than sixty seconds since the bullets started to fly—likely *was* less than sixty seconds—though it felt as if a lifetime had passed, and still I had thought of nothing valuable to add to the conversation, let alone *do*. This failing, I realized, was what made me unfit to be either a drug lord or part of a drug lord's protection squad. Sure, I was a good money launderer—a great one!—but when it came to snap decisions in the midst of chaos, I was all in on the less stressful part of the business. There was nothing now to do but wait for the cops to come—

"Police—" Pablo grunted, echoing my thought.

"Here any minute now, boss."

"OK." Pablo nodded again. "I'm ready," he said and, to my horror, the two chefs lifted Pablo, who stoically allowed it, and started to move him toward the kitchen's exit.

"What are you doing!" I swatted Enio's shoulder. "You move him you risk his life!"

Never swat a bodyguard. I cradled my jaw where Enio had landed a nice, hard jab as he replied, "I don't move him then we risk the police handcuffing him on the way to a hospital. You want that, asshole? Move your ass."

So, I did.

Enio was first out the door, looking left and right as if he was going to cross a street rather than on the lookout for a van filled with shooters to make another pass. Another of Pablo's guards sat in the driver's seat of one of the blue Town Cars, the engine running, and a second stood at the back driver's-side door, holding it open, waiting for its passengers. Enio kicked a large, black leather bag toward the chefs and then motioned them to load-in Pablo.

"Other side," he barked at me and my body must have gone into auto pilot. I can't imagine what else propelled me into the wide-open outdoors where assassins were on the prowl. I must have set a world record for scooting around a Lincoln Town Car and getting inside. To this day I have no memory of opening the door and closing it behind me.

The backseat was crowded—me, Pablo, Enio tight next to each other—and as soon as Enio had slammed his door, the driver sped off, toward the airport, I assumed. "We need to get him medical attention," I said to Enio. "He needs to see a doctor," I appealed to the driver, a man shorter than Enio but with the same muscular build, a full head of dark brown hair and a painstakingly trimmed, chinstrap-style beard. I tried to remember his name— "Francisco! He needs to see a doctor."

Pablo replied, chuckling, "I need to see a tailor. Three thousand dollars for this suit and I think it will go into the garbage." He sighed. The suit was certainly a write-off, though Pablo's bleeding seemed to be staunched. And he seemed only exceptionally tired. "Do we have a doctor, Enio?"

"Rafael's uncle. He called him to meet us at the plane."

"Always good to have a doctor in the family." Pablo smiled. "And he has money? Rafael? For the police?"

"More than enough. We shouldn't have any trouble from them."

Pablo took a moment to close his eyes and rest before he asked his next question. "The men? We did not leave behind our men—"

"No," Enio said, which I had to believe was a lie. There were five of us in this Town Car. We were three short, by anyone's count; three dead, we'd been told, and there was no second blue car anywhere to be seen, no lead car in this race to the airstrip.

I tried to put it out of my mind, the thought of three bodies in black suits strewn and bleeding and abandoned to rot in the hot sun in front of Restaurant Palominos, though I took some comfort that my *rat-tat-tat*-rattled brain was returning to rational thought. A whole picture was starting to come into focus—five of us, a little more than half of our party of eight, had just survived an assassination attempt. Or, at least, five of us had survived so far; a doctor was meeting us at the airport to see to Pablo. Importantly, I was among the survivors. We were fleeing from the police, who were going to let us get away because there was more than enough money in the black leather bag Enio had kicked into the restaurant kitchen to keep them from asking questions. And now my jaw, where Enio had landed his blow, was starting to throb; even my physical senses were returning.

The burning questions that remained unanswered were *who did this*, and *why*, and I was recovered enough to figure that out as well. "Some of the men, in the human trafficking trade?" I said to Pablo. "They were put out by the way you handled the situation."

Pablo attempted a shrug, but I could see that it cost him. He waited until the grimace had faded from his face to answer me. "I thought there might be enough upset to try something like this."

I looked out the Town Car's window, at the scenery speeding by. We were moving so fast that, in my memory, there were sirens accompanying us.

"So, you knew someone might try to kill you, and you walked right into the middle of it anyway?"

Pablo was slouched low in the seat and he looked up at me from the corners of his eyes, showing me surprise, and some contempt. "Do you let fear keep you captive? Is that who you are?"

I wasn't sure how to respond. "Yes!" I wanted to scream at him, but I knew that would only further disappoint him.

Our driver skidded to a stop, far too close to my Gulfstream for my comfort. My pilot, Amelie, thudded down the stairs—a thundering sound far too angry for someone as tiny and trim as Amelie to have made under normal circumstances—and met Enio and the driver as they carried Pablo into the plane. She was not escorting them but taking her share of the burden for Pablo's upper torso from Enio and for herself. This was not, I thought, what she had signed up for when she came into my employ. I was sure I was going to hear about it later. For the moment I wondered only who had called her and put her on standby for our speedy arrival. Our emergency departure. I knew I hadn't had the presence of mind to do it.

A second car pulled up next to us, a black, S-class Mercedes sedan, skidding with as much urgency as we had. An older man in a gold golf visor and a yellow Ban-lon shirt turned off the car's engine and retrieved a brown, alligator leather case before he got out.

"Rafael's uncle?" I asked him.

"*Si.*"

"Follow me," I told him, leading him up the Gulfstream's stairs.

Only at the top, while I waited for Amelie to finish navigating Pablo into a seat so the doctor could move into the cabin to attend to him—while I stepped out of the way of Enio and the driver as they rattled their way back down the stairs—did I turn to look back and notice that the trunk of the Town Car was popped wide open. Three bodies were crammed inside. Enio and his colleague were maneuvering them into the cargo hold.

"Jesus Christ," I groaned.

"Not to worry," I heard Pablo say as the doctor used a small knife to start a tear, so he could rip open Pablo's linen shirt. "I will do my best to be careful with your plane, Clint. Doc, yes? We will not get much blood on my friend's leather?"

Amelie came to stand beside me, and I moved subtly, to prevent her from looking out the door. "What's next, boss?" she asked.

Chapter 4

Wʜᴀᴛ *was* next?

It crossed my mind, as it had frequently over the last several weeks, that I was in the wrong line of work. Laundering drug money is all fun and games—and the perks are hard to beat: I have my own *private jet*, for crying out loud—until someone opens up on you with an AK-47.

I'm fine with the morality of what I do. I'm working strictly within the law of supply and demand, doing just what any good capitalist is supposed to do and, man, I've always been a believer in the free-market system, exactly like almost every politician strutting around Washington, D. C., save maybe the leftie contingent which was, admittedly, on the rise in 2009, but we'd yet to see how that was going to work out. When what you're supplying is drugs, however, it doesn't matter how successful you are at your business because when people find out what your business *is* it's like you've been invited to the White House, but instead of shaking the First Lady's hand you grabbed her by her boob. Drugs are bad! Drugs kill! Drugs make nice people turn to a life of crime just so they can get their next fix! *Just say no!* Right. As if drugs are the only product in the market that are bad for you. Ask Mitch McConnell how many innocent people were killed last year after someone decided to have a couple swigs of good old Kentucky bourbon at their local pub and then drive home. Ask Paul Ryan if it pricks his conscience that motorcycle accidents accounted for over five thousand vehicular deaths in 2008 alone. No, I'm not a saint, but I'm not a hypocrite either.

Anyway, I don't particularly want to go to jail— I've already done two short stretches; neither one for anything remotely to do with drugs, by the way —but jail is a risk I can rationalize because I can take precautions against it. I work smart, cover my bases, and spend most of the year at my home in Mérida, Mexico, where I not only donate lavishly to local pols and police but fund in its entirety a private school for disadvantaged kids. I'm not the only one who has a vested interest in making sure I stay in business.

I've found a decapitated body in my bed, and a dead, deadbeat lawyer in his office. I've faced down a manic if minor drug dealer with a rifle pointed at my chest. I've even survived a previous assassination attempt—with Pablo, as it happened—in which the worst thing that happened to us was that the car we'd been riding in, Pablo's fresh-from-the-factory Cadillac Escalade, was totaled. I was well aware there was some danger involved in my chosen profession.

But the automatic guns this afternoon in Sonora —*rat-tat-tat rat-tat-tat rat-tat-tat* still reverberating in my brain—the unqualified violence of it, the disregard for collateral damage, the three dead bodies below us in my cargo hold—

"Water," Rafael's uncle barked. "Can I get some water?"

Both of the bodyguards standing over Pablo and doing what they could to assist the doctor who was digging a bullet out of Pablo's chest—his left pec where it had lodged, blocked from doing deeper damage by the thick wad of cash Pablo kept in the wallet he wore in his inside jacket pocket—looked to me.

"Yeah. Yes. Hot or cold?" I asked, shaking myself out of my reverie, making my way to the galley without waiting for an answer. There was no one else on board to get the water. Enio was holding Pablo's arm, encouraging him in tones I can only describe as dulcet, still sweating from the stress of watching the doctor plunge a needle into Pablo's exposed muscle to administer a regional pain block. The bodyguard who'd ridden shotgun —a stocky guy with the usual manner of a fellow with an itchy trigger finger, so far as I was concerned—was sitting beside the doctor, calm now as that proverbial cucumber, keeping the wound open with a retractor so the doctor could work unhampered on finding the buried bullet. The driver —whose name I still had trouble remembering... Francisco!—was pacing the aisle as best he could, three steps up and three steps back, sniffing as if he was, startlingly, holding back tears. Amelie was flying the plane. *That* had been a negotiation.

"I will help your friend, yes," the doctor had said, "but we must remain on the ground!"

"We have to get going… we have to take off," Enio had insisted.

"No!" the doctor had countered.

"Why?" Enio had asked. "Will the altitude hurt Pablo? If we are up in the air, will it lessen his chances of recovery?"

"No!" the doctor said again.

"Then let's get out of here," Enio decided.

"I have other patients, waiting in my office, damn it," the doctor swore. "I am not going to Mérida this afternoon!"

"How much?" I stepped in, drawing out my wallet and starting to peel off bills. "A grand? Two? And when we land, you stay on the plane and I'll have my pilot turn it around and bring you right back home."

The doctor paused for a second before he relented. "Two," he'd told me.

"Done," I'd replied. It had been my finest moment. As soon as I'd handed the doctor his bribe, I felt the muscles in my legs go slack and I slumped into a seat far from the surgical area around the patient.

"Hot," Rafael's uncle called back now.

My legs still felt weak, but I fumbled in a cupboard, found an ice bucket and stuck it under the spigot. The hot water on my plane was nearly boiling the minute it came out of the tap—a fact

I knew from burning my finger several times before it stuck that the water was going to be boiling in any case—and I thought about an old joke I'd once heard as the bucket filled: *Hot water, hot water! the doctor called. What do you need it for? the nurse answered. I'm making tea, the doctor replied.* It was the first time I'd had a thought that didn't involve *rat-tat-tat*, which I thought was progress.

"*Mierda!*" I heard Enio cuss, and Pablo emitted a sharp groan in the same moment I felt the turbulence hit us, the plane bouncing in a pocket of air, once, twice—

"Shit," I said as scalding water splashed out of the bucket and onto my belly. It was the best ab workout I'd ever experienced; the ultimate in isometric exercise. "You OK back there?" I called.

There was a pause before the doctor replied, "OK!"

Enio added, softly, for Pablo's benefit, "OK, OK, OK..."

I made my way carefully toward the back of the plane, water sloshing in the ice bucket, wary of hitting another air pocket. I arrived at the patient's side just as the doctor extracted a pair of long, slender tweezers from Pablo's chest, the bullet triumphantly in its teeth. Pablo grunted, only the second sound I'd heard him make during the entire ordeal. "Where do you want this?" I asked, indicating the bucket.

"On the floor." Rafael's uncle gestured at a spot near his foot and, when I'd placed the bucket there, dropped the bullet and the tweezers into it. A few moments later, as he prepared to close Pablo's wound, these were followed by the retractors. As he took them from the bodyguard's hand, I noticed a tremble in both men's hands. The doctor took another moment to let his hand grow steady again.

"I would like a whiskey," Pablo said. "If it's all right with you, doctor."

The doctor nodded. "I would like one too."

"Coming up." I retreated once more to the galley, followed closely by Francisco. "All around?" I asked him.

"*Qué?*"

"*?También tendrás uno?*"

"*Sí, sí.*"

I poured a healthy shot of Bushmill's in a tumbler and handed it to Francisco, who tossed his head back, his long hair flying and greasy with sweat, and drank it in one gulp. He winced as it burned all the way down, then held out the glass for more.

"You see?" he asked me as I poured. "Do you see what he did? He stabbed him with the"—he moved the fingers of his free hand in a scissoring motion—"stabbed with the, what do you say, *ojotos*." He tossed back the second shot. "Tongs," he clarified. "He almost kill him. Almost kill the boss."

Francisco sounded almost boastful about it, but I put that down to nerves. "No, no." I shook my head even as I thought, *so that was why Pablo cried out.* "We hit a rough patch, it wasn't his fault."

Francisco snorted. "We are back there, holding open the boss's skin so the doctor can jab around inside him and I am thinking, this bastard doctor kills the boss and I will kill him, and it is one of ours. His own bodyguard the one who tries to kill him." That he laughed then was disconcerting—weren't bodyguards supposed to be more stoic or self-contained than this? But what really made me frown was the small amber vial he pulled out of the front pocket of his dark suit pants. He swiveled around me, pushing himself into the far end of the galley so he could snort his coke in relative privacy. "Want a bump?" he asked.

I had set out four additional glasses on a tray, intending to pour out shots into each of them and take them to the back of the plane. Now I sat the whole bottle down on the tray. "I've got to get this drink to Pablo."

I was back to worrying my original thought: how suited was I for the business I was in? How long could I last, working with people who would even consider taking the life of a doctor who was doing a service for *us*?

Importantly, except for Alvaro—who, as I said, I'd assumed was an outlier—I'd rarely known anyone in the drug trade to actually *do* drugs. And I thought it was a particularly egregious failing for a bodyguard. "If we get boarded and the feds find that shit on you, they could confiscate my plane," I said as I turned and walked to the back of the plane.

The doctor had finished his handiwork by the time I got back there. He was packing his alligator leather bag, rummaging in it, looking for a slender amber-colored bottle of pills. "Antibiotics. Twice a day until the bottle is empty, and do not fail or he could get an infection and that would not be good."

He held the bottle out to me, but Enio snapped it out of his hand. "If he gets an infection, I will be the one to tell you."

"Here we go!" I sat the tray on a table, filled the tumblers and handed one to Pablo.

"I raise my glass to you"—Pablo indicated the doctor—"and Clint." He reached out to clink my glass.

Pablo threw back his drink, coughed as it slid down his throat. I thought I was the only one who noticed how intently Francisco watched as Pablo clutched at his wound, at the pain the coughing was causing him.

But then I saw Enio watching Francisco too.

Chapter 5

You never realize how much you miss your home until you can't go there.

I was sitting in the kitchen at Pablo's hacienda outside of Mérida, longing for the colonial I'd so lovingly restored in the heart of Yucatan's White City, so named for the gleaming white brilliance of most of its ancient buildings and the fastidious cleanliness of its streets and boulevards. I wanted a shower under my own rainforest showerhead. A beer in a lounge chair in the botanical garden I'd made of my patio. A dip in the blue water of my own pool. It would have made me sound like a whining kid if I'd let myself go on about how homesick I was—barely home from a week's exile in Miami, to keep me out of the way while Pablo cleaned house. Even so I hadn't been able to spend time in my own place because Pablo had me flying all over Mexico to attend the funerals of those he'd cleaned up. And I hadn't been to my school even *once* since my return.

"Pablo," I tried to reason with him without pulling punches, in the direct manner both of us generally appreciated, "why would they want me dead? I'm their launderer too. They were after you. They're not going to be staking out my house, waiting for me to come home."

Pablo wasn't having it. "Too dangerous, Clint. Too dangerous. You'll stay here, with me. I can take care of you."

Of course he could. Every time I looked out the kitchen's French doors there was yet another bodyguard I couldn't name. Neither Enio nor Francisco were among them, having been dispatched to the favored local funeral home to deliver the bodies of the fallen and arrange top-of-the-line funerals for Pablo's dead soldiers. Still, I could have made a game of it, counting the security personnel who patrolled the perimeter of the property, ever alert, their automatic weapons swinging at their sides. I counted twenty-three until I grew bored with the game. And the echoes of the *rat-tat-tat* the sight of so many AK-47s conjured in my ears grew too unbearable.

I called Pedro, my houseboy, and had him pack a bag for me—fresh clothes and favored toiletries. I might be Pablo's houseguest—"indefinitely", as he put it—but I wanted at least my own toothbrush. Pablo sent a couple of the guards to my place to pick it up. Wouldn't even let me ride along, and I knew enough to stop pleading. Pablo was right—the bullet that had hit him had caused merely a flesh wound—and even wounded, even as he lay in pain on the enormous, satin-draped bed in the master suite of the hacienda, resting and recovering, no one thought to argue too robustly with his directives. He was a small man, and a giant; he'd been brought to his knees by an assassination attempt and he was less shaken than I was.

Not that that was a hard thing to be. If even the sight of the AK-47s made my ears ring with the horror of their noise, might that be a sign of PTSD?

There was a pad of paper on the counter of the island where I sat—a small, square tablet of the sort the housekeeper could use to make a grocery list—and a crystal container of the Waterman pens that Pablo preferred. I got up from the leather-covered stool where I was perched to retrieve the pad and one of the pens and started making a list.

1. Pablo – king of kings; ruler of the whole of the Yucatan, Quintana Roo, Campeche, Tabasco, and most of eastern Chiapas.

2. Luis – Oaxaca, and the western portion of Chiapas that Pablo granted him after a dispute in the early 1990s ending with war and a wedding—Luis to Pablo's sister, María Isabel, now deceased; "royal" union.

3. Lucas – another heavy-hitter, top man in Veracruz as well as Puebla.

4. Felipe – Tamaulipas, DEAD.

5. Mateo – Nuevo León who, per pick-up schedule, is either set to inherit Felipe's old territory or supervising operations there as a

sort of interim manager. Going to get ugly if Pablo tries to take Tamaulipas away from him? Unless, as a border state, he was in on the trafficking as well?

6. Tomas – force to be reckoned with: the states of Morelos and Mexico, which includes Mexico City.

7. Andres – Querétaro, Tlaxcala, Hidalgo.

8. Joaquin – Guerrero.

9. Eduardo – Michoacán, Guanajuato, San Luis Potosi.

10. Martín – Jalisco and Colima.

11. Jorge – Zacatecas and Aguascalientes.

12. Roberto – Sinaloa, Nayarit, a slice of western Durango, and southwest Chihuahua.

13. Juan Manuel – most of Durango, Coahuila, and southeast Chihuahua. Coahuila: border state – which side is he on?

14. Matias – Sonora and northern Chihuahua; some relationship with American rancher/ranchers; DEAD.

15. Emiliano – Baja; DEAD

16. Alvaro – last and, as always, least; once Pablo's protégé, thought reign over Quintana Roo was the least he deserved, wife from Chetumal. DEAD.

I underscored the words "DEAD" several times. It suited that the pen I'd chosen was filled with red ink.

The territories I outlined didn't correspond, of course, exactly to the official geographical divisions of the country. There was some friendly overlap, a few not-so-friendly turf wars—which Pablo sought to mediate through the periodic council meetings he hosted at his bunker—and there was also a great deal of inter-territory commerce depending on what grew best where, who manufactured which drug, who had the most efficient access to move product from areas further south. Pablo had put none of that sort of information at my disposal—he'd always told me that the less I knew about how the drug-end of the cartels operated, the safer I would remain. No need for me to have access to the inner workings—know how the sausage was made—in order to do my job.

Still, I knew the identity of the big shot in every state—this I *had* to know—and I sat at Pablo's kitchen counter trying to parse out how the territories were going to be reorganized now that three of the biggest shots, Felipe and Matias and Emiliano, were no longer in business. Would their territories be reassigned, possibly to a neighboring lord? Would some local up-and-comer emerge in a leadership position and take over? Would the territories be consolidated, or broken up among several claimants? The more I puzzled over the fate of the now-leaderless territories, the surer I was that we were headed into one hell of a corporate shake-up.

And that I really wasn't entirely sure I wanted to be around for it. I did the math—always my strong suit: in one year I'd cleaned up well over two billion dollars for the lords—and made a cool one hundred and forty-six million for myself. I was an extremely rich and still relatively young man—hadn't yet celebrated my thirty-fifth birthday, though that was coming up. Why push Lady Luck into a corner? Exactly one-quarter—four out of sixteen—of the drug kingpins I'd started working for just about one year before were now deceased. The mortality rate in this business was off the charts.

Much of any decision I made would, of course, depend on if Pablo would *let* me leave my job. Finding another bank through which to accomplish the laundering might be, as I've said, less of a problem than it would have been if all this hadn't been happening in 2009, when banks all over the place were looking for business to keep themselves afloat. The staff I'd brought in to help me with the collection and transfer of funds— Tim, my second-in-command; and new-hires Oscar and Isaias, who'd worked for me for only six months so far but had proved themselves to be loyal and smart and, importantly, discreet—could keep their jobs even if I no longer wanted to keep mine. If I could find another amenable banker on the US side, they could run the operation without me. The fact that I had engineered a business in which I was so clearly disposable was a blessing in this context, although pretty much a curse if Pablo was the one who decided he didn't want me around.

And what would my partner say? Jack Cohen was my childhood best friend, my brother-from-another-mother, and my partner at Citizen's National Bank of Miami. I was stationed in Mérida, in charge of bringing in the steady business and keeping our Mexican partners happy, and Jack was stationed in Miami, in charge of the management of the assets we bought on behalf of the kingpins, as well as the expansion of Citizen's National, buying failing banks and growing our presence in cities and towns all over south and central Florida. The more banks we bought, the more dormant accounts we accumulated—and it was through dormant accounts, abandoned by the elderly or infirm, that we transferred our Mexican clients' funds. Our electronic manipulation of these accounts caused their owners no problems —the funds were theirs for a matter of seconds before they were transferred out again and into cartel-owned ones with dummy names—and my cut was transferred directly into my fat account, right off the top.

So far, we'd neatly avoided any uncomfortable queries from auditors by being scrupulous about our in-house accounting, and by having David Cohen, Jack's father, in our corner. The bank Jack and I now co-owned had been in the Cohen family for generations, and—though David had recently retired from banking after suffering what had turned out to be a relatively minor stroke—

his pristine reputation, as well as his fraternal relationships with the guys at the Fed, kept the bean counters at bay.

Jack, I was fairly sure, would, in the end, support any decision I made about continuing our relationship with the drug lords, but he would bitch like hell about it until he knew I was dead serious and he didn't have a choice. On the other hand, Jack's mother, Candace, wanted us out of the money-laundering business worse than she wanted the Japanese beetles out of her prize rose garden.

These were the things I was thinking, idly doodling on my list with the red pen, when my cell phone rang. "Speak of the devil," I said when I answered it. "How's Rudy?" I asked. Jack, the happiest of single men, had recently acquired a steady boyfriend, the first one in all his thirty-four years and, from all indications, he was head-over-heels, a state in which none of us had ever seen him. It was fairly disconcerting for all of us to watch him like this.

"Rudy's fine," Jack answered and then, because he couldn't help himself, he *giggled* and added, "Rudy and I are just fine, fine, fine."

"Well, ain't that a kick in the head."

When Jack didn't take my bait, I understood that this wasn't just a casual phone call, a routine check-in. "What?"

Jack sighed. "Yeah, Clint. See, the shit has kind of hit the fan up here…"

Chapter 6

THIS was going to kill me.

I had asked Pablo's nurse if I might have five minutes with him, if she thought he was up to it, and all I wanted to do, now that my request had been granted, was to tell him about the shit that was spattering all over Miami. Pablo wanted to wax philosophic, which was something he could do for hours if he was in the mood. I knew he was genuinely concerned about my safety, but I had a small suspicion that part of the reason he wanted me in residence at his hacienda was for the company. Not that this didn't flatter me, but it wasn't the right time for that.

"You know, Clint, I have no children," he said when I walked into the master suite. He was lying on his back, on top of a pale, sage-green satin comforter, against a towering pile of hand-embroidered pillows. Dressed in a pair of silver-colored cotton lounge pants and a thick, white Egyptian terry cloth robe, sash unfastened, his sixty-year-old, still-in-enviable-shape abs on display. He had his right hand over the patch of gauze on his chest.

"Yes, I knew that, Pablo."

"I have no son…" He sighed.

"No, well, you wouldn't—" *If you have no children
…*

"A man comes so close to death"—he lifted the hand from the patch of gauze and made a lazy, vague circle with his wrist— "he thinks of things like this…"

Oh, my God, I thought. *The assassins didn't get me, but Pablo's going to do the job.*

"Clint, tell me… how is your school?"

"Well, I really haven't been able to get there lately —"

"This is your legacy, this school. You are a smart young man, to make such a legacy. All those children you give the gift of an education—you will have many sons."

"I never thought of it like that—"

"Tell me, how much money do I have now?"

It seemed an abrupt change of subject. "Cash? On hand? Or assets—"

He made another circle with his wrist, this time extending his forefinger, as if to more clearly define the radius. "All of it."

I laughed. "A shitload, Pablo."

"Tell me."

I sighed. "Jack and Xavier"—I always added the latter when I spoke of our purchases on the cartels' behalf; Jack was more or less a cipher as far as the lords were concerned but, even in drug circles in a foreign country, the name of the famous Florida lawyer Xavier Sousa, my long-time mentor and former lover and forever dearest of friends, evoked dignity and trustworthiness, and brought an approving nod—"Jack and Xavier have put most of your money into real estate. As you know, it isn't exactly a seller's market in the U.S. these days, so we're getting you some awfully good deals, mostly foreclosures we're buying directly from other banks." *Other* banks because, among the practices that kept the auditors off Jack's back was our willingness to spread around the wealth that we, among few banks in those days, seemed to enjoy; we at Citizen's National bent over our collective backs to offer the flexible terms that allowed our mortgagees to keep their real estate. The auditors ate that right up, and it didn't hurt our local reputation or our chances of getting into heaven either.

"And how much? How much is it all worth?"

"All together? Several developments in central Florida, an industrial park outside of New Port Richey, a couple of high rises in downtown Miami, a mall in Jupiter and one in Boca... An estate in Palm Beach we remodeled into a high-end nursing home—I can't tick off all the properties for you, Pablo, but what I can tell you is that we started with about two hundred million and we should be able to quadruple that, or better, in a couple of years."

Pablo let out a laugh. "I will own Florida before we are through."

I smiled. "You might."

"We will have to expand into, what is it, the next state up? Alabama?"

"If that's where you want to go. However, I might recommend Georgia. Atlanta's a very nice city."

"And who is managing all this property in America for me?"

I had to be careful about how I phrased my answer. I'd thought about this; if I decided that I really did want to leave my current position in Pablo's organization, I knew my best shot for getting his approval to do so would be to position myself as the very best candidate to manage his growing roster of assets in the states. Working with engineers, surveyors, contractors, decorators, scouting out and training key management personnel to keep my creations running smoothly —this was where my abiding passion lay. The most satisfying work I'd taken on in the last several years had been restoring the gorgeous colonial I called home, as well as the three adjoining ones I'd purchased a few streets over and renovated into the Aj Tz'ib Academy—*aj tz'ib* being the Mayan word for scribe—my school for the least among the Yucatan's residents, the Mayan kids who huddled on the lowest rung of Mexico's socioeconomic ladder. The school was my passion, my pleasure, my homage to the love of my life, the beautiful, young Mayan man, Taavi, who'd inspired me to build it. Who died too young.

If I let myself, I could spend several hours mourning Taavi, and I did not let myself do this often. I willfully switched my thoughts back to Pablo's assets.

Barring this dream job of managing those assets myself, I thought that Charlotte Cruet, the beautiful felon who'd been turning my head for a full year at that point, could fit the bill. She was smart enough to have embezzled a million bucks from under my nose, and scrappy enough to have succeeded as a construction worker, specifically as a member of a demolition crew, when her confession, and subsequent felony conviction, prevented her from the work she really wanted to do. Which was teach. As long as her probation prevented her from leaving the state of Florida—and becoming my employee at Aj Tz'ib—hiring her to manage the cartel's U.S. holdings was the second-best option. She was also seductive enough, with her faint smell of roses and fresh-cut pine, to have turned my head so sharply in the first place. I had always been comfortable with my identity as a bisexual man; never dreamed that I would be willing to choose one over the other. But, once, I had chosen—Taavi. If Charlotte would have me now—if I could ever get her to truly forgive me for forcing her to turn herself in when I found out about the missing money—it would take me a New York minute to settle down with her. Hiring her to manage the cartel assets in the states would keep our lives entwined. And yes, I did think Charlotte could do anything.

"Right now, we've contracted with a few different management companies to watch over your properties," I told Pablo, "but I think there are more cost-effective options. It's on my to-do list to explore those the next time I'm in Miami."

"Good. Good." Pablo nodded. I thought that this might be the pause I'd been waiting for to segue into telling Pablo about the problems that had arisen up north, to let him know that I needed to take a trip to Miami *now*, but he jumped in again before I could do it and you never want to cut off a drug lord mid-thought. "None of these things, though, are my legacy. A shopping mall is not a legacy. An industrial park, no."

"I don't know if I'd say that... What about your housing developments? You're creating neighborhoods, communities for people to live—"

"Tell me, Clint, what you would think if I wanted to make a legacy as you have done."

I frowned. "A school? You want your own school?"

Pablo shrugged, and then immediately winced and rested his hand again on the gauze. "A school is good. Something like that. Something noble. With my name on it." He pondered what he'd just said for a moment, then added quickly, "Not for my sake, but so the name Navarro lives on." He tilted his head, thinking. "So my father's name lives on. Do you think you could find me something noble?"

"In Florida?"

He started to shrug again, then thought better of it. "Why not? You are an American who has built his legacy in Mexico. I will be a Mexican who has built his legacy in America. It's a fair trade, I think, although I also think you ought to just sell me your school because that is what I would really like to have."

I smiled again. How could I have ever given a thought to the foolish notion that this good man would ever want to harm me? I had to stop myself from laughing out loud: Felipe, Matias, Emiliano. *Perhaps* Alvaro, though having had a hand in that death was something he had always denied. Pablo wanted a gentle legacy—so what if he was a cold-blooded killer?

"I can go to Florida to start looking as soon as you give me permission to leave your compound."

Pablo closed his eyes, to rest for a moment. The conversation was wearing him down. He was soon going to need to sleep again. Dire as the circumstances were in Miami, I was losing the nerve I needed to tell him about them. I wanted him in a good mood when I talked and figured another hour or so until I could wouldn't materially change anything waiting for me in Florida. That was when Pablo opened his eyes and asked, "Why did you want to come in to see me, Clint?"

"Uh. Ah—" I stammered.

"You have a problem, I think?"

I sighed. "I have several, Pablo."

Chapter 7

PABLO insisted on a bodyguard. Or, actually, two. Enio and Francisco boarded my plane behind me. They were dressed today in close-fitting jeans, dark linen blazers under which they wore the requisite holsters, and black tee-shirts so tight you could have counted their six-packs—rather more casually than they had been dressed at the funeral; no less imposing. Once Amelie had closed the door for take-off behind us all, I let the guards head toward the back of the plane and stayed up front in the galley. I knew I needed to provide my pilot the opportunity to have at me about our abrupt departure from Sonora, the wounded drug lord in the cabin, not to mention the dead bodies in the hold. Might as well get it over with. I was, full disclosure, not a little surprised that Amelie didn't just leave me stranded in Mérida after we'd landed from that earlier flight and fully expected, once we were back in the U. S. A., to have to start looking for a new pilot—to have to face the stress of finding someone else to fly my plane back to Mexico. Or, even worse, face the discomfort of flying commercial—which sounded infinitely worse to this spoiled young man.

"So," I said to Amelie in the relative privacy of the galley.

The smile on her face was bigger than Julia Roberts's beaming at Richard Gere on a fifty-foot screen. "Are we going to have some more excitement today?" she asked. As if that was something she was looking forward to.

Lordy, I hope not, I thought. "You never know," I said. And winked.

She winked back and headed into the cockpit.

I had to stand still for a moment to fully absorb the pleasant shock that, like me, my pilot was an unrepentant adrenaline junkie.

"Mr. Kennedy?"

Enio had come up behind me, and I jumped when I noticed it. "Ah—yes?"

"Are you coming to sit down?"

It struck me then that I really wasn't going to like having bodyguards. I'd never gotten along well with babysitters.

"I am—thought I'd get us something to drink first."

"We don't drink on duty. Not usually. The other day, that was for Pablo."

"I understand. Not usual to be in the middle of a shoot-out either." *At least I hope so. Does your partner snort coke on duty very often?* "Soda?"

He raised an eyebrow hopefully. "Pepsi?"

I looked in the mini fridge. "Coke."

Enio shrugged. "Pepsi is better for the soul." I nodded, a little stunned to realize that Enio must be—or must have *been*?—a practitioner of that particularly south-of-the-border blend of Catholicism and native tradition in which drinking *pox* was a key component. *Pox* is, to my mind—and I have had a taste of the stuff—a vile though highly intoxicating swill made of fermented corn mash, and it is supposed to be drunk with a carbonated beverage; the bubbles make the penitent burp, and with the burps, then, evil is released from the soul. At least so goes that particular take on theology. Whether one drank Coke or Pepsi with one's *pox* depended on who was holding forth as head of the congregation—or, more specifically, which brand had secured the cola commission with the locality's political elite. The cola wars in the U.S. have nothing on what goes on in Mexico, a filthy miasma of religion, commerce, and politics as far as I was concerned and, in addition, *pox* is simply a pox in the mouth. I suspected the practitioners started to drink cola with it less for the burps and more to rinse the taste buds. In any case, one drank Coke or one drank Pepsi with one's corn-meal crap, and never the twain shall meet.

"Coke will do," Enio said, and sighed so I would know what an enormous concession he was making. I made a mental note to stock the plane with Pepsi as long as he was going to be among my minders.

I had yet to hire a steward, so I loaded up a tray with glasses and a bucket of ice, several cans of cola as well as a bag of Sabritas *adobadas* chips, and took the whole spread to the back of the plane to serve it myself. The guards accepted my offering and I retreated with my Coke to a seat nearer the front. It was unnerving to be surrounded by people, even if in this case it was only two people, whose sole focus was to watch *you*, keep you safe —perversely, it made me feel more vulnerable to be accompanied everywhere I went by people who were supposed to lay down their lives for mine. I still believed I wasn't the person the assassins were after, but the company of Enio and Francisco made me feel as if I might as well have a big red target pinned on the back of my dove-gray linen jacket.

I was sure Pablo had to know more than he was telling me about the attempt to off him—and that, even as we flew to Miami, he was putting a plan in action to take revenge—but I couldn't keep myself from obsessing about *who*. This evening, as Amelie lifted the plane from the runway and banked left, heading north, I was glad for the distraction. Anything to keep my mind off what waited for me when we touched down. I pulled out my list of drug lords to work on the puzzle.

There were twelve cartel chiefs left alive in Mexico—twelve apostles, I thought—and when you crossed Pablo himself off the list, because of course he wouldn't put a hit out on himself— eleven suspects.

I discounted Luis, the Oaxaca-area lord. He was Pablo's brother-in-law, the widower of a sister Pablo still talked about as if he'd adored her. Even though I knew full well that Alvaro had had his own brother-in-law killed at one time, I also knew that Alvaro had been a homicidal hot head. He'd been nothing like Luis, who was more like Pablo himself—elegant and even-tempered, as drug lords go.

That left ten, and I easily discounted Lucas in Veracruz and Tomas, whose territory included the jewel of Mexico City. They were the oldest of the lords, both early mentors of Pablo's and his friends for forty years. They were men who in any other field of endeavor would already have long been in happy retirement, content to spend their vast fortunes on cherished grandchildren and doting wives, playing nine holes in the morning and watching the sun set over their vineyards at night. They each had sons—five between them, if I was remembering correctly—and the sons might grow rash in their ambitions sometime in the future, but not while their fathers were alive and in charge.

I was down to eight. Andres, Eduardo, Jorge, Roberto, Joaquin—of these five men, only Joaquin in Guerrero struck me as a potential candidate, and that was because he had always impressed me as too timid for his line of work. Bullies are always timid, overcome with self-doubt and nearly effortlessly triggered to react by anyone who contested their opinion of themselves. Joaquin was the bully of the bunch, far more like what Hollywood imagined at the helm of a drug empire than the actual cartel bosses I'd come to know. He couldn't be ruled out, but I would have to determine if that was only because, of all the bosses, I personally liked him least.

Martín, the master of Jalisco and Colima, could be worrisome. I had suspected for a while that he not only sold drugs, but indulged in them himself, and copiously, from the abundant supply available to a man in his position. You're around the drug trade long enough—and I had been around it for only about a year at that point, keep in mind—you find any number of merchants sampling their own wares. Usually, however, drug *users* came from the lower end of the organization's ranks, the most disposable of a lord's soldiers. Seldom did you find a success story on the order of Martín's that included such a personal weakness.

Even so, even with these reservations, I kept returning to the final two lords on my list, Mateo and Juan Manuel, the kings of border territories, respectively Nuevo León and, at least temporarily, Tamaulipas for Mateo, and Coahuila belonged to Juan Manuel. Though they were both survivors of Pablo's border raids—his "housekeeping" exercise—it seemed to me that there were no more logical suspects in the assassination attempt than these two men. The primary quest in any investigation boiled down, always and inevitably, to "follow the money" and, in this case, the questions of who had the most to lose/who had the most to gain were answered resoundingly with the names Mateo and Juan Manuel. I revisited the idea that these two were also involved in the trafficking business, though wouldn't Pablo know if they were? Wouldn't he have cleaned up their territories too? Mateo and Juan Manuel were still very much alive.

So far as I knew.

And hadn't Pablo assured me the housecleaning was over? He must have thought that was true, or why would he have let me return to Mexico?

I was doodling again on the list with the red pen I'd inadvertently swiped from Pablo's kitchen, and I startled when I sensed someone looming over me.

"What the fuck, Francisco?" I practically threw myself on top of the list to cover it. Not that the list was something I didn't want him to see, I just can't stand it when people read over my shoulder. It's rude, a huge invasion of privacy. Even for body-guards whose job description includes getting all up in your business.

"What are you doing?"

I sat up and straightened the small sheet of pa-per in front of me, as if to demonstrate I wasn't hiding a damned thing from him. "Trying to fig-ure out who tried to hurt Pablo."

Francisco nodded, sucking on his right canine tooth where a portion of an *adobadas* chip was stuck between it and the molar behind it. "Why you're doing that?"

I shook my head—wasn't it obvious? "Why wouldn't I be doing this? I care about Pablo and someone recently tried to kill him. I'd like know who so we can make sure it doesn't happen again."

Francisco had loosened the glob of chip and he picked it out of his mouth, rolled it around be-tween his fingers, and flicked it on the floor. I suddenly wanted to kill him. "I think this thing you are trying to know is above your pay grade," he said. At that moment I had very little doubt that I could kill him with my bare hands.

Chapter 8

THE past always comes back to haunt you, and I was walking right back into mine. Miami is like the loose-cannon cousin you can't wait to see at the family reunion because you know you're going to have a hell of a lot of fun with him—you're going to drink too much and dance on too many tables and shock the aunts—and then the next morning, nursing your hangover and accepting forgiveness from the indulgent elders, you can't wait to escape for one more year of tranquility until you see him again the next summer.

I'd never actively disliked my hometown—I actually loved my crazy cousin a great deal—but Miami had become, over the course of my enforced vacation there just weeks before, a mess of romantic disappointment (the aforementioned stunner, Charlotte), actual bodily mutilation (Jack's asshole brother, Abe, currently in prison and missing the little finger on his right hand), heartbreaking health issues (Jack's father, the beloved David Cohen, and his continuing recovery from his stroke), unanticipated responsibility (Elmer Collier; put a pin in that name), and potential legal liabilities of the sort that weren't going to be solved by greasing the palms of a few *policías* or sucking up to the local *políticos*. This had all taken place on American soil, and skirting the law in the U.S.A. is always complicated.

Jack picked us up at the airport, slightly put out that he'd had to leave his sporty little car in his garage and borrow his father's sedan for the errand—even if the sedan in question was a shiny, stone-black 7 Series BMW. Jack drove, I rode shotgun, and Enio and Francisco—the guys with the actual guns—sat in the back, hampering our conversation. I told Jack more than once that anything he wanted to say to me he could say in front of my bodyguards, but spelling it out for him —saying outright that I'd learned from Pablo the way to deal with bodyguards was to treat them as part of the furniture—seemed boorish. Neither one of us had the hang of dealing with a security detail.

We drove straight to Xavier's office building, a gorgeous Art Deco-inspired tower in the heart of downtown Miami, and took the elevator to the conference room on the twenty-third floor. Xavier's secretary asked Enio and Francisco to have a seat in the waiting area and all but body-blocked them from going into the conference room with Jack and me; she'd been Xavier's secretary for going on twenty years and was adept at organizing the subtleties of lawyer/client/hired-goon relationships.

"May I bring you gentlemen anything? Coffee, tea, water?" she asked after she had ushered Jack and me inside.

"Martini and Xanax?" Jack replied.

"Coming right up."

"You're more stressed out than I am."

"You're wanted for murder, Clint."

"He's been invited to come in and answer some questions, that's all." Trim, tidy, well-dressed, unflappable Xavier, smelling of a cologne that had a bottle price more than the average monthly mortgage payment on a comfortable, middle-class house, entered the conference room. His clients relied on him for his level head, and loved him for his innate ability to cool their own often excitable response to any legal trouble they'd got themselves into. Never more than today had I appreciated him for these very qualities.

"Oh, thank God," I said, rising and gratefully letting Xavier embrace me. "Sanity!" I turned to Jack: "No more histrionics."

Jack ignored me. "It's bad, isn't it, Xavier? Tell him."

"It isn't good," Xavier conceded, his calm making me feel as if I might be imperturbable about the not-good circumstances too.

I sighed. "Then let's just deal with it."

Xavier sat down at the head of the conference table. Jack took the seat to his right and I took the one to his left. I was put at even greater ease by the clean mahogany table in front of us, the utter lack of paperwork; surely really serious matters required documents—warrants and subpoenas and such. "All right. First things first," Xavier said, folding his hands on top of the highly polished wood. "The police are investigating the murder of Jessie Coulter."

Jessie Coulter was a sleaze bag, a low-rent lawyer who made the bulk of his money taking guardianship of the elderly and/or infirm who had no living relation to look after their interests. Perhaps unsurprisingly, given the median age of its residents, there were any number of such cases in the state of Florida. Coulter took good money from the state for this work and increased the amount in his pocket with the kickbacks he received from the subpar nursing homes and other care facilities into which he stashed the poor bastards who fell under his legal stewardship. I'd made Coulter's acquaintance when he tried to hijack the guardianship of one Elmer Collier from my hands. Elmer was the grandfather of an old employee of mine, a young man who'd died an untimely death involving roller blades and a 1970-era dune buggy on Collins Avenue in South Beach just—what was it? Two weeks ago. I'd made a promise to the grandson about taking care of Elmer and I intended to keep it, which had led to a confrontation with Coulter. When I'd gone to meet Coulter at his office, to try to talk sense into him, I'd found him at his desk, his head mostly on his body but most of it spattered on the credenza behind the desk.

"Clint left that office as soon as he saw Coulter was dead," Jack offered. "Of course he had nothing to do with it, and there's no way they can connect him—"

Xavier cut him off. "What I *know*"—he said pointedly—"is that the police found documents on Coulter's desk that indicated he was ready to take the fight over Elmer Collier to court. He had yet to file against Clint, but—"

"Clint, you see those papers on his desk?" Jack asked. "You didn't think to look, or Pablo's man who took care of Coulter didn't think to look? Can't imagine Pablo's going to be happy about that—"

"Jack!" Xavier slapped the mahogany with an open hand, and then quickly regained control of himself. "In any case, the police now want to interview you, Clint. I suggest that tomorrow I arrange a date for the two of us to go meet them on their terms, and you simply tell them the truth."

Jack refrained from laughing, but only because I kicked him under the table. "Do the police, Xavier — Did the police say anything about a meeting with me? That Coulter had a meeting with me on his calendar for that night?"

"Did you?"

"Do you want to know if I did?"

"So, this could be a sticking point?"

"Only if the police have evidence of it."

Xavier sighed. "I'll see what I can find out. I hate to say it, but I think your more immediate problem is that somehow Donna McAdam got word of the police investigation—"

"The woman at Sunshire?" I asked.

"The Managing Director of Sunshire Elder Care Home," Xavier corrected.

"Whirlwind of energy and self-righteousness," I told him. "And I trust her completely to take excellent care of Elmer."

"I fear the trust isn't mutual, Clint," Xavier answered.

"Say again?"

"She's contesting your guardianship. Seems she thinks someone who lives out of the country isn't appropriate—"

"I have a condo in Miami—I maintain a residence here—"

"And you're not a relative—"

"Elmer doesn't *have* a relative. If it isn't me looking after him, then it's the state, someone like Jessie Coulter who's going to stick him in some shithole and pocket the difference—did she take that into consideration? If the state gets hold of him her fancy nursing home loses a customer, a very rich *comatose* customer who's not going to be able to complain about being moved to a shithole and I'll be goddamned if I'm going to let Elmer live out whatever little is left of his life in a place that stinks of urine and boiled vegetables. Eddie would roll over in his grave... he'd fucking *haunt* me if I allowed that for his grandfather—"

"I think it may be more personal than that, Clint."

"Personal?" I shook my head.

Xavier rolled his eyes.

"What? Xavier, *what*?"

"Ms. McAdams thinks you live a profligate lifestyle—"

"What the hell does that mean?" Jack piped up.

"Decadent, Jack. Recklessly spendthrift," I explained to him, and then, to Xavier, "What business is my lifestyle to her?"

"None," he hastened to confirm, "except for the party you threw for Eddie."

"It wasn't a *party*, it was his, what do they call it? It was his 'celebration of life' and I probably spent less on it than a funeral would have cost, but it was what Eddie would have wanted, and it was a lot more fun, and we raised almost a hundred thousand dollars for the Miami AIDS project that night—"

"And you held it at Club Boi," Xavier pointed out.

I was completely baffled. "I did."

"A gay dance club..."

"Yes. Eddie was a gay man who liked to dance— most of his friends are gay men who like to dance —"

"And then there was the coven of lesbian witches who took over the dance floor at midnight—"

"They were Eddie's friends, and they conducted a service in his honor, and that's religious freedom, Xavier. We have religious freedom in this country!"

Xavier looked at me as if I were eight years old. "You know full well that depends on what religion you're talking about. And you know as well as I do that her concern about the unconventional components of Eddie's services are only covers for her primary complaint."

I narrowed my eyes. "Which is?" I needed to hear Xavier spell it out.

"That you're gay."

I sat quietly, letting it sink in. It had not, for years and years, been particularly hard to be a gay man in Miami. Gay men were not only pillars of the community here, but pillars of the city's economic structure. Now the Managing Director of a nursing home was going to refuse to care for a dying old man because—

"Well," Jack offered, "as Clint is always saying, he's *not* gay. He's bi. He's always been up-front about that."

Xavier offered him a weak smile in return. "I don't think that's going to help his cause, Jack."

Chapter 9

I left Xavier's office feeling like a man without a country. In Mérida I had my beautiful home, my school for the Mayan kids from which I derived more satisfaction than most human beings could hope to have in a lifetime, and a job in a violent business that was increasingly putting me in the line of fire. In Miami I had a comfortable if plebian condo, a possible dream job managing—and renovating!—the drug lords' US interests, proximity to a woman who might change my life if she'd ever give me the time of day, and the law all over my ass. I felt as if both cities were my home, and that neither of them were. *Breathes there a man with soul so dead...*

In Miami, however, I also had the Cohens—David and Candace, my parents in all senses but actual blood; my mother's former employers who had, even when my mother was still alive and working as their indefatigable housekeeper and Candace's personal assistant, never treated me as less than their third son. I also had a string of prestigious alma maters on my résumé—schools I'd attended on the Cohens' dime, though that was indicative only of the hard cash they'd been happy, even eager, to invest in me from an early age; it in no way illustrates the depth of affection —of real *love*—among us.

As Jack pulled David's sedan through the gates of their Spanish-style estate and started up the curving driveway to the house, I felt the tension in my shoulders give way. The sight of Candace's climbing roses, the blooms nearly encasing the massive wooden front doors, made me grin as if I were a kid all over again. "Hey!" I shouted, out of habit, as I opened the front door, announcing that I was home, leaving Jack to park the car and the bodyguards scurrying to keep up with me.

"Hey, wait, hold up." I nearly skidded on the marble in the foyer, turning and putting out my hands to halt Enio and Francisco. "Shouldn't you two wait outside? You know, patrol the perimeter or something?" I had a lot to talk over with the Cohens and I didn't relish explaining why I had security in tow. I had every intention of coming clean with them about almost everything that was happening in my life, but I saw no reason to alarm them with the tale of the assassination attempt.

Francisco looked to Enio, indicating he would defer to his judgment. Enio stared at me for several seconds, an eternity, before his eyes moved to take in the foyer, the large, sunny, well-appointed living rooms off to either side of it, the staircase that swept up to the second floor, and on to the third. Then he closed his eyes, slapped Francisco's stomach to get him to follow, and went back out the front door.

"Clint?" Candace's voice, cultured even as she was shouting a fishwife's summons at me. "We're in the kitchen!"

Of course they were. The kitchen, state-of-the-art and yet as cozy a kitchen as I'd ever been in, had long been the default room for the Cohen family. They frequently got in the way of the household staff—Candace was a competent cook, though she liked fussing over all of us more than the actual food. Now, Henrietta, the nurse the Cohens had hired to help care for David as he recovered from his stroke, passed me in the hall just outside of the breakfast nook, clearing out to give us privacy.

"Welcome home, Mr. Clint."

"Thank you, Henry."

"Clint!" Candace rushed to give me a huge hug and to hold my face between her hands to kiss me hello—a greeting for a long-lost prodigal.

"It's so great to see you, Candace," I said, and it was, though it had been less than a week since I'd last done that. She was wearing an "at home" outfit as chic as it was comfortable—simple silk slacks in a mustard color, with a matching shell top, and a pair of black patent leather ballet flats with small white bows at the toes. She kissed my cheeks three times—left, right, left—and moved on to hug and kiss Jack, who'd followed me into the room.

I moved across the kitchen to greet David, seated in his wheelchair. The last time I'd seen him he'd not yet been dressing for the day, still wearing pajamas and a robe and fuzzy slippers when he gathered with us in the kitchen. Now he had on white trousers and a light-blue polo shirt, along with his fuzzy slippers, which I took as a good sign his recovery was moving in the right direction. "David," I said, extending my hand.

"Glad you're here, Clint," he replied, grasping my hand with his good one and pulling me to him for a quick embrace, the hand that had been affected by the stroke still resting limp in his lap. "What brings you home again so soon?"

"Well," I started, ready to dive right into my current tribulations.

But Candace stopped me. "Cocktails first!" she announced. For most people, this sort of cheer may have been an indication that she had no idea what was coming. But I knew Candace: she knew my unanticipated visit to Miami meant there was something brewing and she wanted to make sure we were all lubricated enough to deal with it.

"I'd love one of your Manhattans," I told her.

"Aha!" she agreed, and leaned close to me and whispered, as if she was sharing a state secret: "The trick to a good Manhattan is rye whiskey and orange bitters." I laughed because we both knew that the first time I'd heard the secret from her was when I was around twelve years old and she gave me my first bartending lesson.

When Candace had the four of us settled around the breakfast table with our drinks—David's glass filled with only a half ration—I spilled the beans. Jessie Coulter's death wasn't a surprise to either David or Candace—they'd read something in the newspapers about an attorney who'd been murdered in his strip-mall office, though there were small gasps when I told them I'd found the body the night it happened but had quickly left the scene of the crime without reporting it to the police. And they remembered that I'd taken over guardianship of an old employee's grandfather when the employee had been run over by a dune buggy, and they were shocked that *anyone* would think I wouldn't be a most responsible guardian. They were furious when I told them that, among the reasons that Donna McAdams at Sunshire Elder Care Home wanted me removed from Elmer Collier's case was that I was gay. Candace, in particular, took it hard.

"That miserable little bitch," she fumed.

"Yes," I agreed.

"She will never know the comfort of being taken care of by anyone as wonderful as you two." She waved the diamonds on an elegantly manicured hand at Jack and me.

Jack smiled. "And there's Abe, too. Don't forget Abe."

"Oh, he'll still be in prison by the time I kick," David muttered.

To this Jack objected rather desperately: "He's only going to be in jail seven more years, Dad."

"You never know. Besides, I don't want him taking care of me—"

Candace pointedly cut him off. "In the meantime, I'm still perfectly capable of taking care of others—Clint, you'll call Xavier first thing in the morning and arrange to put me on the paperwork as Mr. Collier's legal guardian."

I shouldn't have even blinked—Candace hadn't —but I did. "Are you sure? You're already busy here, with David—"

"You made a promise, Clint. If your family can't step in and help you keep it, what good are they?"

"I love you, Candace. I don't say that often enough."

"I love you too, dear. Now, David, what are we going to do about the police prying into Clint's whereabouts on the night of the murder of that awful Coulter fellow?"

David took a deep breath while he thought. "Who's the detective working the case?"

I think I did a double-take—at how incredibly foolish I'd been: "I have no idea. I met with Xavier this afternoon and I didn't even think to ask his name."

"Find out. I'll make a few phone calls, see what I can dig up."

"I really appreciate that, David."

In reply he waved his good hand at me, as if there was nothing there to be grateful for.

"Good!" Candace said. "We have a plan of action … I like that. So, now, Clint, I would like you to tell me who are those two good-looking men who've been prowling around the outside of the house the whole time you've been here."

Candace didn't miss a trick. Ever. Though Enio and Francisco hadn't made it hard for her to no-tice them. They'd actually been standing on the patio outside the Cohens' kitchen when Candace brought them to my attention. "I asked you to be discreet," I seethed at them in David's car, as Jack drove us all back to my condo at the end of the evening.

Francisco shrugged. "We are not used to being 'discreet'. Most of the time people, they want everyone to know we are there—they want people to know they are protected."

"I don't want that." I turned around to look at them in the back seat and smacked the console with my open palm, as emphatic as I thought was required.

"We will try to do better," Enio promised.

"Will you, please!" I snapped at them, turning quickly to face front again so I didn't see Enio nod.

I did, however, hear him add, "We could make your problems go away, if you wanted us to do that. One call to Pablo, he will want to know, of course, and approve before we do anything, but we could start with this Donna McAdams, you called her? Start with her and"—he snapped his fingers —"make your problems disappear."

My old friend, adrenaline, propelled me and I nearly spun out of my seat to get my body turned around so I could look him in the eye. It had been Pablo's thugs taking care of my problems—Pablo who'd ordered the hit on Jessie Coulter in the first place—that had directly caused the current problems to roll into my life. "No, Enio. I don't want you to do that. Listen to me: *I definitely do not want you to fucking do that*."

Chapter 10

"DETECTIVE Louis Aiello," Xavier said when I picked up his call early the next morning.

I was still in bed when my cell rang and I threw back the sheets and made my way to the kitchen in my condo, wanting caffeine to focus my brain. My bodyguards were already awake—Enio folding up the sheets and blankets I'd provided for them to use as they took turns napping through the night on the heather-gray sofas in my living room, and Francisco offering me a large mug of already-brewed coffee. My Miami digs are not the perfect venue for any overnight visitor save a hot date, lacking a guest room and featuring only a bath and a half, nor was the place meant to be —it was a classic pied-â-terre and it was being invaded. I was unreasonably irritated when Enio slipped in through my bedroom to use my shower. And that Francisco had rummaged around in my cupboards to find where I kept my coffee and my mugs and the spoon with which he stirred his own cup of joe while he leaned against a counter, watching me talk on the phone with Xavier. I wanted to tell him to go the fuck away, give me some space—but there wasn't anywhere for him to go.

I pushed past Francisco and made my way to the small balcony off the living room where I would have a modicum of privacy. The whole city of Miami was up and moving as early as I was, judging from the parade of cars and the clusters of pedestrians on the streets below; I trained my eyes on the stunning vista of Biscayne Bay beyond. "Did you run the name past David?" I asked.

"I did," Xavier answered, "and he agrees with my take on the matter. Aiello is an old-school cop, a just-the-facts-ma'am type, and there were any number of others who would have wanted Coulter dead, not just you. My information, for example, is that he was attacked a few days earlier by another of his clients, an old woman with a cane, of all things, who got him so hard across the knee that she tore his ACL. That was why he was limping the last week of his life—Coulter's secretary is singing like a bird about how he ran his business, and that's all to the good for you. You need to go into your meeting with the understanding that interviewing you is merely a formality, a lead Aiello's obligated to follow-up, and be straight-up with him."

There were any number of other questions I wanted to ask Xavier, but I knew enough not to do it over the phone. I was living in a world where bodyguards had been assigned to protect me from random attempts on my life, so tapped phones weren't out of the question.

"Meet me at my office at 9:30," Xavier said. "We can go over all this in more detail—your meeting with Aiello isn't scheduled until eleven."

I checked the time on my cell. 8:15. Knowing that I'd have to face the law in just under three hours set the adrenaline flowing, and my breath was short.

"Mr. Kennedy," Enio called from inside the condo.

"What!" I shouted back at him.

"Your shower is free," he said, finishing his toweling off in my living room, stepping into the pants he'd worn the day before. "You want it, or you want Francisco to go now?"

We were scheduled to meet Aiello at the Miami force's headquarters on Second Avenue, so we caravanned there—Jack had picked up the bodyguards and me at my condo, to take us to Xavier's office in David's sedan, but the sedan rolled behind now as Xavier and I drove toward Aiello alone in Xavier's dark-gray Mercedes-Maybach S 560.

"So, I can rest easy, knowing there's no record that Coulter and I were supposed to meet on the night of his murder?" I don't have nerves of steel, but I've been able to keep my cool in any number of tense situations; still, I wanted utter clarity on this point.

"If you'd had a meeting with me, it would be recorded on the calendar on my computer as well as on my secretary's, and it would have been posted on all the partners' calendars too. A matter of being able to coordinate, reaching each other when the need arises and so forth, that's why we do it. Coulter, on the other hand, was a one-man operation with only one computer in his whole office and, as far as investigators have been able to tell, used only by his secretary to receive incoming emails from the offices of certain judges, whenever they assigned a guardianship to him. The rest of his paperwork truly was on paper, as if it was the 1970s in his office, and not well-organized. A great deal of his files were stacked up right on the floor, though the secretary has indicated that was the result of the attack a week or so ago. By the old woman with the cane—remember, I told you. Apparently, she went on a rampage in the office, tearing it apart, and she and Coulter hadn't yet put it back to whatever sort of rights they normally enjoyed."

"No paper calendar?"

"Not so far as I know, Clint."

"I suppose that's the best information we have?"

"It is. And it's good information."

"Rest easy, then?"

I didn't appreciate the pause before Xavier answered, "Yes."

Jack waited outside, in the car with the guards, while Xavier escorted me into police headquarters. I was immeasurably relieved to be shown by an officer into an actual office. I had expected to be taken to an interrogation room, the sort one sees on television, painted puke-green with a single, metal table at its center, a couple of worn, straight-backed chairs around it, no windows but a harshly blinding light above. Maybe decorated with an intimidating two-way mirror. Instead, I was ushered into a rather small, conventional office space filled with an older, untidy but well-maintained wooden desk, several padded leather chairs for us all to sit in, bookcases and file cabinets lining the walls and the bright Florida morning sun shining in through a rather large window behind the desk. The detective himself struck me as a little young to have been described as "old-school", possibly in his middle forties, trim and with most of his hair still on his head, dressed in crisp suit pants and a dress shirt, albeit with sleeves rolled up over hairy forearms, and no tie.

"Detective," Xavier began with introductions, "Xavier Sousa."

"Mr. Sousa," the detective replied.

"This is Clint Kennedy," Xavier introduced me.

"Mr. Kennedy." The cop extended his hand, further putting me at ease. Cops, I had to assume, wouldn't so readily shake hands to greet a person they had a mind to arrest before the end of their interview. "Thank you for coming in. Have a seat."

"Glad to," I replied.

"Mr. Kennedy"—Detective Aiello took a seat himself, referred to a sheet of paper clipped to the top of a manila folder on his desk and placed a small recording device on the table between us—"I'm going to record this."

I quickly looked at Xavier before I answered, "Yes. Of course."

The detective nodded and switched on the machine. "So, you had some dealings with a lawyer named Jessie Coulter immediately before his death last week."

"I did."

"Can you tell me about them?"

"I can. One of my former employees, Mr. Eddie Collier, had asked me to take over the guardianship of his grandfather, if Eddie should predecease both of us. Eddie was killed and, so, I stepped up as I had promised to do—"

The detective held up a hand to stop me. "Just to be clear, when you say Mr. Collier was your employee, you mean he was one of the prostitutes who worked for you when you ran an escort service."

"I did eighteen months in prison after my service was shut down. I have since given up that line of work—"

"What does this have to do with Mr. Coulter?" Xavier interjected.

"As I said, just clarifying," the detective replied. "Go on, Mr. Kennedy."

"Eddie's grandfather, a Mr. Elmer Collier, was mistakenly assigned to Mr. Coulter's guardianship after Eddie's death—"

"By Judge Errol Kushner, I believe," Aiello added.

"To my knowledge," I replied. "I've never met Judge Kushner, though he was quick to correct his mistake when it was brought to his attention —"

"Only after Mr. Coulter's death?" Aiello asked.

"Yes," I admitted. "Though I had already challenged the assignment and was certainly ready to fight him about it. Eddie died a wealthy young man, there was no reason for Coulter to have had his grandfather moved from a fine nursing home into—I can't even remember the name of the place where he put him, some substandard dump that smelled of piss—sorry, urine. There was no reason to save money on his care other than to put the savings in Coulter's own pocket, as I'm sure you've found was Coulter's intention. Coulter wasn't going to profit on a sick old man's discomfort—not on my watch."

"We fully intended to fight him in court over custody," Xavier added, "and there was no reason to think we wouldn't have prevailed."

The detective nodded. "Why was Elmer Collier's care so important to you, Mr. Kennedy? Seems it would have been much easier to have simply let Judge Kushner's error stand. I mean, why would a young man who spends most of his time in his home in Mexico want the burden?"

"I didn't *want* the burden, Detective. But, as I said, I'd made a promise. I intended to keep it. And when I saw for myself the place where Coulter had dumped the elder Mr. Collier, well—"

"You were angry?" the cop suggested.

"I was."

Aiello nodded again, and consulted his notes on that single sheet of paper on top of the manila folder. "You met with Mr. Coulter on Friday, October thirtieth of this year, correct?"

"I did. For lunch, at Cvi.che 105."

"Was that a satisfactory meeting?" the detective wanted to know.

"It was not. Not entirely. Coulter accused me of being a spendthrift with Eddie's estate, so I did find out what the grounds were that Coulter was going to use to fight me. That was helpful, and I felt fully confident that, once the court had a look at the paperwork, it would see that this was clearly not the case. You'll see the same if you have a look."

Aiello nodded once more. "And this meeting at Cvi.che 105? This was the only time you met with Mr. Coulter?"

Xavier had prepared me for the question. I took a breath before I answered—

Chapter 11

"Yes," I said, in answer to the detective's question. And then I waited. And turned over in my head the idea that I hadn't actually just lied to the police. I had never seen Coulter again after our lunch at Cvi.che 105. Not alive. If that wasn't a loophole then, really, what was?

Xavier leaned forward in his chair, reached for a framed photo on Detective Aiello's desk, a pretty young girl with a big grin on her face and a mortar board on her head. "This is your daughter?" he asked.

The detective smiled. "High school graduation, last May."

"She's beautiful. Where is she now?"

Aiello grunted. "St. John's, in Maryland."

Xavier whistled.

The detective nodded. "Tell me about it. But she got a nice scholarship package."

"You must miss her." Xavier said, replacing the photo on the desk.

"Like my right arm," the detective allowed. Then he turned to me. "Again, thank you for coming in, Mr. Kennedy." He extended his hand to me, and I took it, but I still wasn't breathing properly. One of two things could happen now—before he let us walk out the door the detective could instruct me not to leave the state, because he'd want to talk to me again, or he could just let us walk out the door.

"You're most welcome, Detective Aiello," I replied. He released my hand and reached for Xavier's.

"A pleasure to meet you, Mr. Sousa."

"And you, Detective."

My legs didn't feel as if they had bones in them until I was back in David's sedan and Jack was driving us away from the Miami police headquarters on Second Avenue.

"So, all is good, right? We can go back home now?" Enio asked. He was sitting with Francisco in the backseat of the sedan, worrying a wart on the side of the middle finger of his right hand. That's how bored my bodyguards were. Warts were more absorbing than my life. Or protecting it.

"Not quite yet, Enio," I told him. "One more stop."

"The Grove?" Jack asked.

"It's like you can read my mind."

The Grove was where Eddie had bought three small, two-bedroom bungalows, all on the same cul de sac, all in foreclosure. When the dune buggy had taken him out, he'd been in the process of renovating them, to get them on the market to flip. As the executor of Eddie's estate, I had opted to follow through with his plans. I was in town, so I figured I'd stop by to check in on what kind of progress the contractor was making.

Also, the contractor had hired Charlotte to work on the demolition crew. If I was lucky, she'd be there, demolishing something besides my heart.

When Jack pulled into the cul de sac, it looked deserted. The residents of the two other houses in the small semi-circle neighborhood—the houses that were occupied—must have been at work on this mid-Fall weekday, like all the good people of the world. There were no cars at either of the houses. No cars in sight at all, as a matter of fact, just one yellow truck with my contractor's name and logo on the driver's door.

"What the hell?" I muttered.

"Like you always say"—Jack shrugged—"you take your eye off a contractor, he disappears."

"Shut up."

I walked through all three houses before I found two of my contractor's workers—a young Hispanic man I had never seen before out back, on the patch of concrete that passed for a yard, loading up the last scraps of a demolished carport into a dumpster at the side of the house; and a woman sweeping up the last dust of old drywall where a wall had been taken out to open up a tiny kitchen and provide the house with a more modern open floor plan.

The woman was Charlotte. She looked up when I entered. "We finished demo this morning," she said.

"I see," I replied, but all I saw was a stray strand of glossy hair sticking to the sweat on her neck.

"What are you doing in Miami? I thought I just got rid of you last week."

I laughed. Her remark hurt and pretending I found it funny softened the blow. "I'm just in for a day or two. Business."

"You're a busy man, Clint."

"Look, Charlotte, I have a proposition for you—"

Now it was Charlotte's turn to laugh. "You proposed last time we saw each other, remember? Remember what I said?"

"A *business* proposition."

Charlotte leaned on her broom. "Go on."

That she would show even this much interest surprised me, and I said as much.

Which made her laugh again. "I'm working construction, Clint, but not even *construction*. I'm the destruction crew. I smash walls with a sledgehammer and clean up the mess that's left when I'm done. I never build anything. All I'm good for is tearing shit down and, thanks to you, tearing shit down is the only work I can get. Whatever you have on your mind, it's gotta be a step up. Of course I'm interested."

That set me back. It took me a good four or five seconds—an eternity—to form my reply. "OK. Good. Let's go get a drink and I'll tell you about it."

"Let's not. I'm on the clock, Clint. Just tell me what's on your mind."

I took a deep breath. "I want you to come and work for me."

"In Mexico? We went over this already. I'm a *felon*. I can't leave Florida."

"In Florida. The job is in Florida, right in Miami … you can work from home, or we could get you an office space—probably an office space would be better. I need someone right here to manage, you know"—I waved my hands around to try to encompass the whole tiny house we were standing in—"things like this. Oversee renovation projects I've got going on right here."

Charlotte grinned. "So, I'd be, like… My boss's boss?"

I walked toward her, and she didn't shy away. "You'd be the boss of every crew I've got working for me. Charlotte"—I took her filthy, dust-covered hands in mine—"I have almost two hundred million in renovation projects going on right now, and more on the way. You'd be in charge of them all."

Charlotte let my hands rest on top of hers, but she made no move to return the embrace. "Two hundred million?" The idea made her laugh again.

"Yeah." I laughed with her.

"God, think of how much I could embezzle with a portfolio like that—"

"Stop it," I told her, and she had to lean on me because she was giggling so hard.

"Why would you even want to hire me to do a job like that—"

"Because anyone who can steal that much money out from underneath my nose can do anything," I replied, sincerely. "I mean, anyway, it wasn't as if I didn't find out. And get the money back."

She fell into my arms then, shaking with laughter. It was the first time I'd ever really held her. She felt soft and warm and tiny and absolutely unbreakable. We were two criminals, Charlotte and I, and, if we joined forces, we might well be able to rule the world. Or, at least, a little portion of Florida, and a bit of Mexico too.

She looked up at me, from her perch in my arms, and when she parted her lips, I thought I might have an orgasm on the spot. I thought she was offering them for a kiss. But she'd parted her lips only to ask me a question. "How much does a gig like this pay?"

"Ah, uhh, I haven't decided. How much would you like it to pay?" So much for any notion of being a great negotiator; I'd give her the moon if she asked for it.

Charlotte slid out of my arms and straightened up. Brushed some dust off the front of her shirt. "I was making twenty-five thousand a year when I worked for Abe at the bank. It'd have to be more than that."

I was shocked, though I tried not to show it. Twenty-five thousand? A year? No wonder she'd stolen from me. "A lot more," I told her.

"Enough to pay off the mortgage on my dad's house. And my student loans, while we're at it. You know that's the only reason I got involved in Abe's scheme in the first place."

"More than enough to do those things," I assured her. Ten times as much. At least. With bonuses for bringing projects in on time and under budget. "We can work it all out. Will you come and have a drink with me—we can work it all out over a drink."

I thought she was on the verge of saying yes. Anyway, her mouth was starting to move into her dazzling smile. Then, in an instant, she was— Not *frowning*. Squinting. With disbelief, shock. Suddenly looking as if she was really pissed off.

"What? Charlotte? What?"

She shook her head, then turned it to look at her left arm, and she stared at the blood that was blossoming on the sleeve of her tee-shirt.

Chapter 12

THE next thirty seconds passed like a fever dream. Charlotte slumped in my arms. I didn't miss the second shot, a thud as a bullet hit the far wall and embedded itself in one of the studs—or maybe that was only an echo of the one that had hit Charlotte, another sort of *rat-a-tat-tat* in my own brain? I heard my own screams—"Jack! Call 9-1-1!" Then Enio was running into the kitchen through the front door and taking Charlotte from me, lowering her to the floor. Jack hot on Enio's heels, pulling his cell phone from the pocket of his blazer. Francisco skidding to my side from what seemed to me to be out of the blue—I was no longer able to keep track of the activity around me, focused as I was on Charlotte, but I saw him swat Jack's phone out of his hands, heard him shout, "No EMT! No police!" The confusion on Jack's face that turned almost immediately to anger as he bent to pick up his cell—"The fuck, Francisco!"—and, again, "Fuck!" when he saw the screen was shattered. My desire to ball up my fist and smack Francisco with it, and how I was distracted by Enio picking Charlotte up off

the floor and starting out the front door with her
—"Flesh wound only. No police. Clint, get the
door to the car, we take her to your apartment."
Scrambling to follow Enio and Charlotte out the
door—"What do you mean, 'flesh wound only'?
We have to take her to the hospital!" Enio not
missing a beat—"No hospital. Come." Me flying
out the door to get ahead of him to open the back
door of the sedan. Jack tripping as he stumbled
to keep up and get behind the wheel. Cramming
myself into the back seat with Enio, Charlotte between us. Francisco standing outside of the car,
saying something about having to clean up before
we go. Me reaching up to grab his lapel—"Get
in the fucking car *now*!" Francisco yanking open
the front passenger side door and sliding into the
car like a petulant teenager. Charlotte's hand
reaching out to cover mine, squeezing my fingers,
smiling as she saw she'd dripped a few drops of
her blood onto the sleeve of the dove-gray jacket
I'd thrown on again that morning, and catching
my eye—"Sorry. But, really, I think I did just get
grazed. I'm OK. Really." Feeling as if I was going
to die of an adrenaline overdose.

"What the fuck do you mean you have to go back
and get rid of the *body*?" I had Francisco backed
up against the cupboards in my condo's kitchen,
the collar of his dark linen jacket wrenched in my
hands, whispering and hissing with such force
that my spit was hitting him in the face. "What
fucking *body*, Francisco?"

Francisco stood erect, with a passive expression on his face while I ranted. Enio was in the living room, ministering to Charlotte's wound, and Jack —who was a whole lot less cool about our afternoon adventure than even I was—was pacing between my kitchen and my living room like a caged and terribly confused feral cat. No one was trying to restrain me. It was only when I paused to catch my breath that Francisco deigned to give me a reply: "I saved your life, Mr. Kennedy. A little respect."

Jack seemed to skid to a halt. "*How*? How did you save Clint's life?" he demanded.

I let go of Francisco. "Yes. Tell us how."

"The man who was trying to kill you?" Francisco shrugged. "I killed him."

The man who was trying to kill you.

It hit me suddenly, like a ton of fucking bricks: a man had been trying to kill me.

I was the target.

Quite possibly I'd been the target all along, back at Restaurant Palominos.

Not Pablo at all.

Francisco straightened out the collar of his jacket—brushed it where it had wrinkled in my fists. "I saw the man in the backyard, the one sweeping up the mess from the carport, and he pulled a gun. I saw him fire in through the kitchen window, so I shot him. This is how I saved your life."

I wanted so many more details, but even I could recognize that the salient one at this point was that when we'd fled the scene, in my panic to attend to Charlotte's wound, we'd left the body of the assassin behind, in the back yard of the bungalow in the cul-de-sac in the Grove.

A body that, when found, could be traced back to a piece of real estate I controlled.

A detail that would no doubt make it into Detective Aiello's dossier on the Jessie Coulter investigation, much to my detriment.

I also imagined the case Donna McAdams would try to make against a gay *murderer*, which would certainly not be in Elmer's best interests.

I glanced over at Charlotte, who was watching Enio unravel a strip of gauze around her upper arm, to bandage her wound. She caught my eye and, as if reading my mind, said, "Probably best to go back and retrieve the body, Clint."

Charlotte, I decided, was the one who should be working with the kingpins, not Jack or me. She was the only one of the three of us who'd been both shot and able to keep her head about it. I might have been more in awe of her cool if Jack hadn't squealed like a puppy whose tail had just been stepped on that *he* was certainly not going to be among the party returning for any *body*.

"Clint…" Enio made a final tuck in the gauze and, rising from Charlotte's side, gestured to me to follow him. "…you and me."

"You and me *what*?"

"Francisco, you stay here with the girl and the coward," was his reply.

Jack was indignant as he squealed again. "*Coward*?"

"Enio, surely you and Francisco would be a better choice to go and deal with this—"

"And leave your friends here, in your home, without protection?" he asked.

"Well." I seriously considered this option before replying, "No." And I added, "I guess."

Enio looked at his watch. "Let's go now, before any of the neighbors start coming home from work. While the neighborhood is still empty."

"Wait," Charlotte called. She stood and fished a set of keys out of the front pocket of her overalls and shook them at us. "I'll go with. Someone's got to finish cleaning up the carport and drive the truck back to the contractor's office."

Enio drove David Cohen's sedan back to the Gove, and Charlotte rode shotgun. I sat in the back. I wasn't shaking, or in any other way physically impaired so I couldn't drive, but I knew that I wouldn't be able to focus my mind on anything other than the fact I was about to go remove a dead body from a murder scene. I would have been useless—I would have been *dangerous*—behind the wheel.

Charlotte, on the other hand, sat up front, chatting easily with Enio, giving him directions and pointing out turns with her clipped wing. Halfway there she had him stop at a Walgreen's where she hopped out of the car and returned with a bag filled with half a dozen boxes of cornstarch—a purchase that struck me as odd, but no stranger

than any other thing that was making up my
bizarre day, so it didn't occur to me to comment.
At the house, she jumped out of the car and
flagged Enio in as he backed up into the driveway,
inching the trunk of the car as close to the body as
was physically possible, cutting the wheel so any
activity at the back of the car would be camou-
flaged by a huge hibiscus—in case anyone in the
nearby houses came home from the office while
we were at work. She fished a blue tarp out of the
back of the contractor's truck for us, and handed
Enio the box of disposable rubber gloves she'd retrieved from behind its passenger seat before she
started to load the rest of the demolished carport
in the dumpster at the side of the house.

The young Hispanic man I'd seen earlier lay face
down on the patch of concrete that took up almost
all the backyard. I was rather grateful I couldn't
see his face. That I didn't have to look into the
cold, dead eyes of the man who'd tried to kill me
a few hours earlier. Francisco had made a clean
hole in the back of his head and he, in turn, had
bled freely all over the concrete pad. "Oh, my God,"
I sighed.

"Put these on," Enio replied, waving the box of
gloves at me.

You don't realize what the phrase "dead weight"
really means until you try to move a dead body.
At least I hadn't. The young man couldn't have
weighed more than a hundred and forty, maybe a
hundred and fifty pounds, but moving him was a
struggle, even if all I helped to do was spread the

tarp out beside him and roll him onto it. Then I stepped out of the way and watched while Enio wrapped him up as neatly as a butcher wraps up a couple of strip steaks in brown waxed paper and tied the package up tightly with some woven blue nylon rope in lieu of butcher's twine. It was when Enio popped the trunk of David's car and motioned for me to grab an end of the package and I squatted to hoist my end that it felt as if every abdominal muscle in my core ripped through my abdominal wall.

Chapter 13

I wanted to lean against the sedan and catch my breath after we'd loaded the body into the trunk and Enio had tapped it so it closed—but I didn't know the protocol. Was it gauche in the criminal world to touch the outside of a getaway vehicle with tainted rubber gloves?

"Here," Charlotte said, holding open a clean plastic garbage can liner for me. When I didn't respond she added, "Your gloves. Take them off and put them in here."

I had started to shake so badly that it was a struggle to remove them but, when I had, she dropped the garbage bag on the grass beside me and walked over to the large red stain on the concrete. She had two boxes of the corn starch she'd purchased earlier at the Walgreen's under her free arm. She ripped the top off one, and then the other, and sprinkled the powder over the blood. The powder began absorbing the red puddle even as she jogged back to get the other boxes. Even before she could dump them over the puddle too.

She gave the cornstarch a few minutes to do its work, then brought two shovels from her truck and began shoveling up the pink goo from the concrete. When she'd removed most of the goo, she retrieved a gallon bottle of degreaser from that magic truck of hers and squirted it over the still pinkish concrete.

"Watch this," Charlotte said after she'd given the chemical a few minutes to work on the stain. "The best blood remover I've ever used."

I closed my eyes, not daring to ask the burning question: *Just how much call do you have for blood remover?* Then I watched as she scrubbed—and only lightly—with the broom she'd been using on the kitchen floor when we'd first arrived at the house. I watched in real amazement as the stain lifted from the concrete like a miracle.

"*How do you know this*?" I asked out loud.

Charlotte shrugged. "You'd be amazed at the sorts of things you have to clean up on a demo crew," she said, and shrugged again. The concrete pad, except for a few small cracks and a worn edge at the far end, was so spotless it looked as if it could have been poured the week before. "We were supposed to clean this up anyway."

Charlotte hosed off the pad, then helped Enio bag the broom, the shovels, the empty cornstarch boxes—all the *evidence*—into a couple of huge, industrial-grade trash bags she produced from her well-equipped truck, and Enio stashed them in the trunk of David's sedan with the body of the would-be assassin.

Thinking of him that way was helpful. *Would-be assassin.* There was no reason to feel guilty about tossing this guy into the trunk of a car, right? He'd tried to kill me. He'd actually shot Charlotte. He was trying to do harm to me and mine. Or, anyway, someone I hoped to make mine.

Had hoped to make mine.

"I'll meet you back at Clint's after I've dropped the truck off," Charlotte said and climbed into her truck. She waved to us with her good arm as she shifted into gear and drove away.

I admired Charlotte for her cool in handling the disposal of the body, but I didn't like it. There were crises one could be commended for taking in stride; dumping a dead body wasn't, I thought, one of them.

I certainly wasn't taking it in stride. I'd been able to do nothing more than lean against David's car, watching the action; except for lifting the body into the trunk—something I did only in deference to Charlotte's wound—she and Enio had done most of the work. I was still shaking so badly as she pulled out of the cul de sac I could barely wave back.

"What... What do we do now?" I asked Enio.

Enio stood in front of me, feet spread, hands on hips, and shook his head.

"Shouldn't we, you know... get out of here?" I tried a laugh. "Make our getaway?"

"We have a problem," he replied.

"Oh." I nodded. *Tell me something I don't know.* "OK. Is it, like, where to drop off...?" I gestured at the trunk with my shoulder. "Where to drop off our friend?"

Enio shook his head. "That I can take care of. Our problem is that I can find no gun."

It took me a minute. "No gun?"

"What did he use to shoot your girlfriend with? I have looked and looked and there is no gun out here."

"Well—" I tried to think, an act of will that made me squint, and caused a low-grade headache to fester right behind my eyes. "Maybe Francisco picked it up before we left."

Enio frowned. "And put it where?" he asked.

I glanced at my watch. Four-thirty. People were going to start coming home from work soon. "How the fuck should I know, Enio?"

Enio looked at me for a second—a passive glance, no acrimony, no contempt, only sorrow. "You shouldn't," he replied and headed into the demoed house.

"What are you doing?" I asked, and followed him. Not out of curiosity, but because I thought I could hurry him along in whatever task it was he'd left undone inside.

Enio stood in the open space of the kitchen, in about the same spot where Charlotte and I had been standing when she was hit. He looked toward the open window in the back, through which the bullet had come, and then turned in a slow semi-circle, scanning the walls until he found what he was looking for. He approached one of the studs in the front room where new dry wall was scheduled to be installed and pulled a folding knife out of his back pocket. He used it to pry a bullet out of the beam. He studied it for several seconds before walking back to where I waited at the back door to show it to me too.

"I... I don't know anything about guns, Enio. Bullets, anything like that. What are you trying to tell me?"

The frown Enio had worn on his face for the last hour or so deepened. "That I think you and I should keep it just between the two of us that I have the bullet," he said.

I emphatically did not want to go with Enio when he disposed of our friend in the trunk, and he —as emphatically, though, to my mind, less reasonably—did not want me to return to my condo. "People in and out, a real crowd compared to the usual traffic at your home, I'll get my hands on the security tapes from your lobby once I do get you home," he said vaguely, and I was too physically shaken and emotionally shook to argue with him.

"There are security cameras in the elevators too," was all I said.

"Good to know," he replied and dropped me off in front of Xavier's building. "Go and have a nice drink with your friend. I don't know how long I'll be, so maybe you'll have dinner with him here too, all right? I'll call you when I'm ready to pick you up —you can meet me right here on the street again, yes?"

I nodded, wondering at all I still did not know, and all I did not want to know. I figured one of the things Enio wanted to get out of my visit with Xavier was my face on his building's security tapes. A witness who could alibi me for this terrible day's late afternoon hours, should I need it. The problem was that I didn't *want* to see any-one, even Xavier. Maybe *especially* Xavier, as I was feeling an intense desire to share the day's events—to burden another person with trying to help me figure out the puzzle of who would try to kill me, and why. And I knew without being told that the less people who knew about the events of the afternoon, the better the chances were that the information would stay among only the people who already knew it.

I walked through the soaring, white-on-beige-on-ecru lobby of Xavier's building, the heels of my shoes clicking across the white marble floor, and took an elevator to the top floor, the exclusive restaurant Xavier maintained there for his plea-sure and convenience.

Besides, Xavier was an officer of the court; there were things I *couldn't* tell him without causing a fuck ton of problems for both of us.

"Good afternoon, Mr. Kennedy," the bartender said as I sat myself on one of the barstools and pulled out my cell phone to dial Xavier. "What can I get for you this evening?"

I smiled and stuffed the phone back into my pocket. I didn't need to call Xavier because the bartender could vouch for my whereabouts, should that become necessary. I could be alone with my awful thoughts—it felt like the first break I'd had all fucking day.

"What can you get for me?" I mused. Something strong, and bracingly cold. I knew there was a small freezer behind the bar wherein were stored bottles of Grey Goose and Belvedere and Stoli Elit and lots of other even more rare and exclusive distillations, all lined up on racks, neatly on their sides. "Vodka, rocks. With a twist."

"Coming right up—any particular vodka?"

"Surprise me," I told him.

Chapter 14

Jack lay flat on his back, on the sofa in Clint's living room, a cold cloth across his eyes. He'd stopped shaking, but only because he was concentrating on his breathing, a relaxing yogic exercise his boyfriend had taught him and that, initially, he'd dismissed as a bunch of woo-woo hooey; now, he thought—breathing through his right nostril, then his left, then his right again—the technique was going to save him from a full-blown panic attack.

Not that he thought he didn't entirely deserve to have a full-blown attack: in all of his thirty-five years, a life he'd only reluctantly agree had been a pampered one, he'd never been in such close proximity to violence as he had been in that modest little bungalow this afternoon.

And he wanted never to be that close again.

When Pablo had caused his brother Abe's pinky finger to be unceremoniously amputated, he'd been miles away from the jail where it had happened and, even at that distance, the very idea of it had haunted him.

Continued to haunt him.

He and Clint were going to have to have a long talk about cutting the drug lords out of their little American bank.

Jack was so absorbed in counting his breaths—three in and out of the left nostril, then three in and out of the right, and methodically back to the left again—he had no inclination to wonder, or to care, what the other person in Clint's condo was up to.

Francisco, for his part, stayed in the kitchen, out of Jack's way. He'd pulled one of Clint's Heinekens out of the refrigerator and leaned against the counter while he drank it, fuming that Enio had ordered him back to this condo—acting, for all practical purposes, as if he were the one in charge of the operation, treating Francisco like an underling, shaming him in the eyes of everyone in the group. Why had he insisted on both getting rid of the body and protecting Clint by himself? The skinny little coward shaking on the sofa, he wasn't part of the operation—Pablo hadn't said a word about protecting him. Francisco sucked on the beer. Why was he here? It was as if Enio doubted his fitness.

Or his loyalty.

He slammed the green beer bottle onto the countertop and yanked his cell phone from his back pocket. "And so you and the miserable gringo have fixed our problem?" he hissed when Enio picked up.

"Not yet," Enio replied. He was driving, and distracted by the traffic around him. He'd thought that the farther he drove away from Miami, from the city's central hub, the more likely he was to come to some rural, unpopulated area where he could finish taking care of the day's business. He didn't know Miami well, however, and the more he drove the more it seemed he'd entered into yet another suburban circle of hell. Where were all the orange groves that were supposed to be in Florida? "Why are you calling me? Has something happened?"

"Nothing has happened!" Francisco replied. "Nothing is happening! Why am I not helping you to do something?"

"Because someone should be at Clint Kennedy's apartment, in case a killer comes to finish the job and you can take care of him—" Enio looked around, in despair at the vista before him: houses in rows and cul de sacs into the vast distance. No place to bury a body as far as the eye could see. "I will come to Mr. Kennedy's apartment as soon as I can," he growled. "Do your job until then."

"Bastardo," Francisco muttered as Enio disconnected the call. There was no job here in this fancy condo. Enio's attempt to make him think he was doing an important thing, being in this apartment, was weak. What you would tell a child to make him stay out of the way. He reached into his front pocket, pulled out the vial of coke he'd brought with him, and tapped some onto the back of his hand. Almost as immediately as he snorted, the sensation of power restored surged through him. Cocaine was his favorite drug, better than the heroin he sometimes had to substitute if supplies were scarce, and the purity of the stuff he had on his hands was uncompromised—and this was Henri's doing. Henri had no favorite drug, only the requirement that whatever he was ingesting at any given hour be of the highest quality. He'd be seeing Henri again soon, but—he held the vial to the light over Clint's sink and tapped it—not soon enough; his supply was running low.

It never hurt, when one was in a situation of deprivation, to do a little foraging, Francisco thought, and he quietly opened and closed a few of the drawers under the counters in the kitchen, though all he found were dish towels, knives, forks, spoons, a wine opener, and old, paper-wrapped sets of chopsticks like you got with Chinese take-out orders.

He peered into the living room. Jack was still sprawled on the sofa and so Francisco made his way to the master bath. Most people kept their stash of pain relievers and other pills in their medicine chests and the large, mirrored one in Clint Kennedy's bath seemed promising. He rummaged through it now, hoping to find, maybe, some hydrocodone leftover from Clint Kennedy's last toothache... But, no, nothing. Nothing but an oversized bottle of generic OTC acetaminophen and a few individually wrapped cough drops.

Maybe in the drawer of the nightstand? That was another logical place for a stash, though Clint Kennedy's stash seemed to consist of a sleeve of Claritin, an obscene amount of condoms, and every grocery list he'd written for the last several years—beer, bananas, coffee, cracked pepper crackers. He read a few of these missives Clint had written to himself and was about to close the drawer and go look elsewhere for anything more interesting, when he unfolded a larger sheet of paper, the one Clint had taken from Pablo's house and used to sketch out his suspicions regarding Pablo's various business partners.

He was so transfixed by Clint's list that the ringing of the doorbell barely registered. Still, Jack had just cracked the front door and the words "Hey, hi! Clint home yet?" were scarcely out of Charlotte's mouth than Francisco had pocketed the handwritten list, rushed to the living room with his gun drawn from the inside pocket of his dark jacket and had it trained on Clint's two friends who stood—frozen, open-mouthed—on the small, raised, slate-covered platform that served as Clint's foyer.

Charlotte recovered first. "Put that thing away, Francisco. For God's sake, where do you think we are? Tombstone? 1875?"

Jack groaned and resumed his position on the sofa, flinging the cloth once again over his eyes, as Francisco holstered the pistol.

"Give me that," Charlotte said, swiping the cloth from Jack's brow and swinging into the kitchen to freshen it. "What's Clint got to drink in here?"

"Beer. In the fridge," Jack called.

"Heineken!" Charlotte enthused, taking two and, with a toss of her head at Francisco, asked, "You want one too?"

Francisco's lips fluttered into a curl that Charlotte couldn't read—a sneer or an attempt at a grin?—and he reached past her, into the refrigerator for another beer for himself. Charlotte shrugged and skipped into the living room, and Francisco took up his position again, leaning against the counter, cracked his beer and took a healthy gulp of it.

He was itching to have a more detailed look at Clint's list, but what bothered him most—what stayed in his head and gnawed at his brain like a hungry rat—was that Pablo had expressly told him and Enio to not only protect Clint Kennedy's life, but to keep him from trouble in general. To make sure he had what Pablo called "plausible deniability" if the three of them ran into any difficulty while they were in Miami. Taking Clint Kennedy along to dispose of the bod—

It struck him in the face, like that wet washcloth the coward Jack was holding over his eyes while he was draped across the sofa like a southern belle with the vapors: of course Enio hadn't taken the gringo along while he disposed of the body. Mr. Clint Kennedy was alone right now, sitting in some public place where his innocence could be observed by strangers, while Enio did all the dirty work by himself. Enio had purposely gotten Francisco out of the way, was deliberately deceiving him about Kennedy's whereabouts. And that meant he was suspicious of Francisco's abilities to do his job. Or of his loyalty. Francisco took another swig of the beer and felt his teeth grip the top of the bottle, as if in his anger he would bite it off and spit it across the kitchen.

"Hey, Jack," Francisco said, leaning out of the kitchen doorway to look into the living room.

Jack was still on the sofa, sitting up now, his eyes closed and the ecstatic expression of a dying saint on his face while Charlotte stood behind him and massaged his temples. "Ohhhh," Jack cooed, "that feels so good…" he moaned and raised a hand, palm out, to Francisco. Then he extended the forefinger of that hand and waggled it at Francisco to signal that he should not be disturbed. If Francisco thought he could have gotten away with it he would have leapt across the living room and broken that dismissive finger right off his fucking hand.

Instead he forced himself to take a deep breath and said, "I need to reach Mr. Kennedy. I do not have his number in my phone"—and why was *that*? Because he was a bodyguard and wouldn't have expected to be separated from his charge? Because Enio had, from the start, intentionally kept their charge's phone number from him? "I need to use your phone now to be in touch with him."

Jack still did not open his eyes, but Charlotte looked at Francisco. "Clint's all right, isn't he?" she asked.

"Mr. Kennedy is of course all right," Francisco answered, keeping his voice even, forcing a smile, "I need only his phone number to call him and deliver a message." He nodded, and, when neither Charlotte nor Jack responded immediately, he added, "From Pablo."

Jack still hadn't opened his eyes. "Don't stop," he groaned and used one hand to tap Charlotte's idle fingers, moving them over his temple in a small circle until she started massaging him again, and the other hand to point a finger at the coffee table, where his iPhone rested. "It's running out of juice," he said as Francisco moved into the room and picked it up. "There's a charger in the kitchen. When you're done with your call, plug it in so it can charge."

"It will be my pleasure to do that, Mr. Cohen," Francisco said, grabbing up the phone. "That will most certainly be my pleasure."

In the kitchen, he scowled at the cracked screen and scrolled through Jack's contacts until he came to the entry for Clint. He hit the number listed for his cell and held the phone to his ear. "Come on, Mr. Kennedy," he whispered. "Pick up. Answer my call..."

Chapter 15

THE vodka the bartender chose was Stoli Elit, not that it mattered. It was smooth and ice cold and the faster I got it into my mouth the faster it was going to take the edge off.

"Let's do it again," I told the bartender, pushing my empty glass across the black marble top of the bar, toward him.

"Very good, sir."

The funny thing about getting drunk is that, while, in reality, you've more or less abdicated control of your life—"more or less" being highly subjective, depending on the amount of alcohol you've consumed as well as your personal tolerance for the stuff—you *feel* as if you're the king of your dominion: your whole being awash in abiding wisdom and infallibility. Or, as is the case for those of us who aren't either perfect jackasses or committed alcoholics, reality begins to seem—for those few hours of hazy inebriation—*manageable*. The loose ends begin to float together and, if not tie themselves up in neat and tidy end knots, at the very least stop writhing like tortured, venomous serpents, and come to rest in some less troublesome order.

The woman you had hoped would become your lover shows a side of herself that leaves you both baffled and icy cold? Well, better you found out she was too cool a cucumber for your comfort sooner than later, right? I mean, who gets *shot* —even if it's just a minor flesh wound in the upper arm—and then has the presence of mind, or is nonchalant enough, or possesses the god-damned gigantic *cajones* that allow her to clean up the blood of the guy who just tried to knock her off? Sure, Charlotte had tried to rip off my bank for a couple of million bucks, but hadn't she sorrowfully confessed she'd done that only to pay off her school loans and help her father with the mortgage on a modest family house? And only then because Abe had lured her into his embezzlement plot? Wasn't this the same young woman who'd touched my heart with her burning desire to become a teacher? Who'd made that same heart burn with desire whenever she flashed her sunshine smile? Whenever I'd inhaled the innocent perfume of pine trees and roses that swirled around her? Not that I was in the market for a *naïf*, for God's sake—I was a man of the world and I wanted a partner who could keep up with me; what I wanted, if I was being brutally honest, was someone who was *better* than me. Who could walk my same crooked path while still tamping down the worst of my instincts. Was that too much to ask? *Probably*, I thought, dipping my hand into the bowl of peeled, salted pistachios the bartender set out wordlessly before me. *Maybe*, I mused, *I* was the one who'd decided Abe was to blame for Charlotte's transgressions. I mean, she'd never actually told me Abe had initiated their whole nefarious scheme—and I had never actually asked her. I'd just fallen hard for Abe's co-conspirator and let the scenario in which she was blameless be my comfortable default.

The man who'd been, for your whole life, a willing, kind, and generous father figure—indeed, the only *father* you'd ever known—was laid low by a stroke? I tried to be casual about my concern—I had wept with the fear of losing David Cohen only once, in the privacy of a private plane, where no one, save, possibly, the steward, had seen my tears. There was no question that the care his wife, Candace, provided for him was the best her loving heart and the Cohens' vast wealth could provide. And yes, he *was* getting better; I could measure the progress with each visit to their home. Still, if I let myself think about David's recovery it felt as if the tissues in my chest and throat were swelling—as if I were going to be choked by hope.

The profession that had made you an excessively rich man no longer suited you? Had become, paradoxically, too routine and too dangerous, both at the same time, and you wanted out? Between my assistant, Tim, and my banker, Juan Carlos, I had become merely a figurehead in my own money-laundering enterprise. I might have come to accept this state of affairs as satisfactory

—might have found another outlet for my energies: a side business to keep me from being bored silly, preferably in some edgy industry to feed my need for adrenaline—but telling Pablo I wanted out was a stumbling block. I had no idea how he'd take it. Would he *allow* me to leave? For all his pretensions, framing the cartel's business in corporate euphemisms, he was a drug lord. One just didn't walk away from the mob; take a step outside and you became, yourself, a loose end. Pablo liked me, and he trusted me—to the point that he'd asked me to help him create a legacy project for himself on the order of the school I'd created in Mérida. But how far would that affinity stretch if I was no longer part of his organization? Well, that was what Donald Rumsfeld might call a *known unknown.*

You found yourself on the radar of the local police? Because you were linked, however peripherally in their estimation, with a murder? True, the nice detective, Louis Aiello, had seemed to accept the statement I'd *voluntarily* made to him at face value—he hadn't asked me not to leave the jurisdiction, after all, but he also hadn't given me any reason to be relieved that he wouldn't want to talk to me *again.* Not to mention that the simple fact was I *did* have something to hide. I hadn't killed anyone, of course, but I knew a hell of a lot more about the murder than I wanted the law to find out about. Think trying to keep a secret from a detective who's picked up your scent doesn't make for a hell of a lot of sleepless nights?

Then, at last, there was the big, overarching, really killer question: Someone wanted you dead? Well, I could feel your pain. If it weren't for Enio and Francisco, I might actually *be* dead. Strangely, this wasn't, however, the sort of problem that was going to keep me up at night; this was a problem that was both so real and not real at all, and those competing ways of contemplating it rather drained the senses. While it was a dire query, it was also too out of the realm of whatever I'd thought was possible in my life, and I couldn't quite latch onto it as an actual, physical threat.

With this morbid thought my phone rang, as if on cue, while I was finishing my third Stoli Elit. I fished the phone out of my pocket while the bartender was—utterly without judgment—pouring me a fourth. I checked the number—Jack ringing me up. I didn't feel like talking to him anymore than I felt like talking to *anyone* right at the moment, but I answered anyway. "Yeah?"

Instead of one of Jack's standard, snarky greetings—"Yeah, yourself, asshole"—I heard a question—"This is Clint Kennedy?" —rendered with a heavy, hearty Mexican accent.

"Yes, this is Clint, Francisco. Where's Jack?"

"He's here with me, with your Charlotte—she is here too, at your apartment."

"Has Enio showed up there yet?"

There was a pause, as if Francisco was thinking this over. "No," he said. "But he has asked me to come and collect you, and bring you back to your own home."

I didn't relish the idea of being around all those people—Jack and, especially, Charlotte—but I figured, in the end, it was better for me to go back home than to keep hanging around Xavier's restaurant, drinking myself into oblivion. Four Stolis was probably a good limit—and, if I got home and found it was not, there was vodka in my own freezer. Several varieties, as a matter of fact: Ketel One and Grey Goose, and a few fingers of Absolut Citron left in the bottle. And I did love lemon drops.

"OK, Francisco. Come and get me, then."

"Where are you?"

"Xavier's restaurant, but don't worry about parking. I'll come down and meet you outside the lobby."

"I can be there in about"—here again, Francisco paused—"give me half an hour."

"Sure," I told him, and downed the fourth drink the bartender placed in front of me before I hung up. "Yes, well, then"—I held my now-empty glass out to the him—"one more for the road."

"Very good, sir."

"Ver, ver good," I replied, and noticed I was starting to slur my words. Yes, well, then; clearly five was going to be the best I could do about limiting my alcohol intake this afternoon.

Chapter 16

Francisco hung up Jack's phone and tucked it into his back pocket with one hand as he scrolled through the Waze app on his own, looking for the nearest car rental outpost. There was an Alamo on Chopin Plaza. He calculated the distance and, realizing that walking there would certainly make him late to meet Clint, called for a taxi to pick him up at the apartment and drive him to Alamo.

"I have to go out," he announced to Jack and Charlotte, walking through the living room, straight to the door.

"Where's my phone?" Jack roused himself from Charlotte's ministering hands, still rubbing gentle circles at his temples, to ask.

"In the kitchen," Francisco answered as he opened the door. "Charging," he added as he closed the door behind him, bypassed the elevator bank and broke into a run to take the stairs down to the lobby and meet the taxi he'd summoned.

Enio cursed the urban sprawl all around him. Driving aimlessly around an unfamiliar city with a body in the trunk of your borrowed car was not enough to make a seasoned strongman like Enio nervous, but it did piss him off. Enio's nerves were, in any case, made of that proverbial steel, forged in the mean streets of Mexico City, tempered by nearly a decade in the Mexican Army's elite airborne special forces unit, Gafe, where he'd specialized in counterterrorism. The Army had recruited him when he'd been but nineteen, and Pablo had recruited him the day after he'd turned twenty-eight, after he'd become one of the world's most polished killing machines. He'd had to defect in order to join the cartel's forces—and once he had defected, he then knew he would be living the rest of his life outside of the law—but the money Pablo had offered him was not to be refused. And he earned every dollar Pablo paid him—yes, dollars; it was part of his employment agreement that Pablo paid him in American money. It had been no walk in the park to take out those three kingpins who'd run afoul of Pablo's dictates. And Pablo had been pleased with his work—his efficiency and his discretion. But now he was circling the suburbs of Miami, looking for a place with a little privacy, enough to dump a body, and he'd left his primary charge alone and unattended while he did it. Pablo was not going to be pleased about that. Although he would surely give Enio a chance to explain himself—a chance to lay out the reasons why he'd had no choice but to act as he had; Pablo was nothing if not equitable. He would give Enio a fair hearing, even if something happened to Clint Kennedy in his absence, before he gave the order for Enio to be put down.

"Fuck," he growled and jabbed his fists on the steering wheel.

The taxi dropped Francisco in front of the Alamo office and he threw a couple of bills at the driver as he exited the car. "Keep the change," he called.

"What change?" the driver called back. "Three dollars? Fucking cheap bastard," the driver shouted as Francisco disappeared through the door.

His hands shook as he stood at the counter, ordering up an economy ride, fumbling through his wallet to come up with his alternate ID and the credit card with which he'd been supplied, stolen from a tourist in Puerto Vallarta only the day before Francisco had been sent to Miami. He held his breath as the clerk ran the card, unsure of what his options were going to be if the transaction was declined.

Francisco was just twenty years old, only a few years from the poverty of his early life on the streets of Tlaxcala and his too-recent transition from street urchin to cartel goon. He could kill a man with ease, but not yet with finesse. Joining the cartel had opened up the world to him, but he still had no idea how the world worked. The stolen credit card was the only credit anyone had ever thought to give him. The only credit he'd ever had to his name at all. He counted the cash in his wallet—he could afford the car for a day if the credit card was rejected, he thought, but he'd been told he'd have to use the stolen card if he needed a vehicle. He could use the card for a hotel room, or a meal, if that was necessary, but his supplier had been very specific about needing the card for a car. He realized he wasn't breathing only when the clerk spoke.

"Here you go, Mr.—" She squinted at his fake ID as she handed him a set of keys. "Mr. Abramson. Our valet will bring it right out from for you." She pointed at the glass front doors.

"Thank you," Francisco told her, slipping the stolen card back into his wallet. "Thank you very much," he said, sucking for air.

Enio wheeled the car hard onto a street called Grenada. He had been driving south and found himself on Ponce De León Boulevard, no longer angry but resolved now in the need to find a new plan of action. Grenada presented itself as a thoroughfare that would allow him to pull over, turn the car off, think, before pointing himself south once again. Unfortunately, following the road put him on the expansive, landscaped grounds of a country club, the pristinely manicured greens of a golf course. He felt his anger rise again, but he tamped it down—by training and temperament he was, after all, a counterterrorism specialist, and he'd been caught in stickier situations than driving around a major American city with a dead body in the trunk.

Fortunately—yes, there was always a silver lining, he thought; a saving grace—he was behind the wheel of David's shiny BMW sedan, a vehicle that was by no means out of place on the grounds of the swanky Riviera Country Club, and no one gave him a second look as he piloted it through a turnaround and back onto Grenada. He was able to pull over a few blocks later, on a relatively less trafficked street called Anderson Road. He turned off the engine and took his foot off the gas pedal, let himself slouch in the driver's seat while he looked around at the neighborhood. Contemplated his next move.

That was when the police cruiser pulled up behind him.

Chapter 17

I left the bartender several bills—which may or may not have all been hundreds—and stumbled out of Xavier's bar and into the elevator to meet my ride outside the lobby. It became very clear that five vodkas was well over my limit when I had to squint to make the numbers on the elevator panel stop moving. So I could find the button marked "G".

"Ground floor," I said out loud, in triumph, after I'd found it and given it a push. I leaned back against the nearest wall to wait as the car carried me to the lobby, but it stopped two floors down.

I pushed myself off the wall, into a full upright and standing position, suddenly embarrassed in the eyes of the two upstanding folks who'd joined me in the carriage—he in a navy-blue suit and rep tie, and she in a beige skirt-and-jacket ensemble and sensible heels. The man nodded to me as they entered, the woman indicated by her averted eyes that she would acknowledge no notice of me at all, and we three, all now turned to face the mirrored doors of the elevator as they closed, again started our descent in the polite silence of the corporate elevator.

The car stopped again after we'd gained six floors. At this stop—my legs feeling a bit like melting gelatin, not entirely capable of supporting my full weight—I reached out and put a hand on the wall to my right, to help keep me stable as the elevator lurched to a stop to admit another passenger. At this stop a janitor, pushing a big yellow bucket of water in front of him, got on. "Sorry," he said, maneuvering the bucket in, "service elevator's out." The man in the rep tie and the woman in the sensible heels backed up to allow him and his equipment room in the car, and the janitor— a middle-aged guy whose graying beard reeked of weed—stood facing all of us as the mirrored doors closed on the elevator once again.

I wanted to point out to him that, by not turning around and pointing himself *toward* the doors, he was violating a sacred if unwritten rule of elevator etiquette, but the smell of his beard, a ripe combination of rotting hay and skunk, made me feel as if I was going to gag when I opened my mouth. I promptly shut it, all but the thinnest slit, breathing through it to avoid taking in the janitor's odor —and that of whatever chemical was swirling in the water within his bucket—through my nostrils. Which might have helped except that the chemical was bleach, or ammonia, something strong and insidious. It entered through my taste buds and the very pores of my skin, and I wretched loudly, causing the man in the rep tie and the woman in the sensible heels to jump forward, out of my way. The janitor pushed himself back into a corner, pulling his bucket with him lest I think of it as a receptacle if I ended up actually vomiting.

My eyes were watery, still seeing double, but I grasped for dignity. I put a finger to my mouth and shook my head, vamping for a moment until I could rasp, "Your cleaning solution." I kept one hand on the wall, for balance, and with the other removed the finger from my mouth and waved it at the bucket. "It's very strong. I'll be fine, but you really shouldn't be transporting *that*"—I waved the finger faster for emphasis—"in a passenger elevator."

That I got no back-up from the man in the rep tie or the woman in the sensible heels didn't bother me. It was enough that the looks of horror, the ones that had appeared on their faces when I'd wretched, softened, and the janitor shifted his position, putting his body protectively between me and the bucket but at last doing the civilized thing and facing the door.

When the elevator stopped once more, three floors down—what felt like another lurch of a roller coaster to my jelly legs—I wretched again. It was another unproductive sound effect, but as awful as it was to feel my stomach contract and the alarming noise to issue from my mouth, I was sure there was no danger of actually making a mess. When the elevator came to a full stop and the doors opened, the man in the rep tie and the woman in the sensible heels and the janitor pushing his precious bucket all raced to get themselves out and wait in the lobby of the accounting firm that was housed on that floor for the next car down.

That was the floor on which Xavier saw me standing alone in the otherwise abandoned car and boarded it.

"Clint? What are you doing here?" he asked as the doors once again closed and I braced myself against the wall for the downward jolt, knowing that the motion was going to make my stomach rise upward.

"I stopped by your place, to have a drink," I told him, forcing out the words in a way that could sound sober only to a man who was very drunk.

"Or several," Xavier observed.

"Yes," I agreed. "Several. What are *you* doing here?"

"Well, Clint, this is my place of business, and I had a meeting with my bookkeeper, and— Nonsense. What's the matter with you?"

"Why should anything be the matter with me?" I countered.

"Well, something sure as hell better be the matter with you—I hope you haven't taken this up as a habit, getting shit-faced in the middle of the afternoon."

"Nooooo..." I tried to laugh as I said it, and then laughed because I realized how ridiculous I sounded.

"Is it something to do with the police? Do they want to talk to you again?" Xavier whispered.

"Nah. No, nothing like that."

"Then, for God's sake, what?" He looked at me, up and down and then once again. "You can't even stand up by yourself."

Even as drunk and unbalanced as I truly was, I knew whatever conversation Xavier and I would, without doubt, inevitably have about the events of the afternoon, it shouldn't take place on an elevator. "Can't a guy have a couple of martinis in the afternoon, after a hard day?"

Xavier sighed. "Are you headed home, Clint? Let me call you a taxi."

"Not necessary," I informed him, still gripping the wall for dear life. "I have a ride on the way. My bodyguard is coming to get me."

"Well, that's fine, I suppose," Xavier allowed, relieved, I think, that there wouldn't be any nonsense trying to talk me out of my car keys.

"Come on, man, you know me better than that. I'd never drive while under the influence, and I am certainly under the influence."

"You certainly are, my friend."

"I do need you to help me do one thing."

"What's that."

"I'm meeting my ride right outside your lobby. Help me get from here to there, if you would."

Xavier shook his head, but I also saw a small smile flicker on his face. "Of course."

Francisco was waiting in the driver's seat of a tiny but tidy dark brown Mitsubishi four-door. He leaned across and swung open the door as he saw me approach, and Xavier poured me into the passenger seat.

"Seatbelt," Xavier said, pulling the strap across my body, handing Francisco the business end so he could buckle me in. "You should take him right home and put him to bed," Xavier said.

"No problem," Francisco replied, which set Xavier off; the phrase "no problem" being one of his pet peeves.

"Are you this man's body guard?" Xavier asked Francisco.

"I am," Francisco replied.

"Then I am here to tell you it is most assuredly not your 'problem' to take him home, it is your *job*."

"Yeah, sure," Francisco replied.

He might as well have said "Duh" for all he indicated he understood Xavier's intent, and Xavier just looked defeated. He leaned over me. "Clint?"

"Yes, Xavier?"

"Go home and take a nap and a shower, in that order. I'll call you this evening."

"I will look forward to it," I told him.

"Jesus," Xavier muttered as he slammed the car door closed.

I remember that I tried to begin the recommended nap immediately. That I leaned my head to rest it against the window and closed my eyes. I remember feeling Francisco pull into traffic and, though my young bodyguard was no mental giant, I remain sure that he waited until we were far enough away from Xavier's building—and, so, any possibility that Xavier would see what he was doing— to whack me across the back of the head with the gun he carried, efficiently sending me off into the oblivion I'd tried to find in the afternoon's vodka.

Chapter 18

Enio looked out the car's back window through the rearview mirror. The police cruiser that had just rolled to a stop behind him was a Florida Highway Patrol guy, not one of the local cops. A lone policeman—and it was a man—got out from behind the wheel. He paused to adjust the heavy belt around his paunch and wiggle his left leg—adjusting his junk—before he started sauntering toward the BMW. Enio leaned over the passenger seat, fishing the registration and insurance information out of the glove compartment—right where David had told him it would be—and flipped through his wallet to extract the Florida driver's license and concealed carry permit Pablo had arranged for him before he'd left for this trip to America. He had just enough time to adjust his sport jacket to camouflage the shoulder holster where he carried his Glock. His paperwork was in order, but no sense throwing his firepower in the cop's face. He was, after all, a brown man in a ritzy, white section of a prosperous city in the state of gun-crazy Florida. The gun was within easy reach, however, if it turned out he had need of it—which he was hoping he did not. He already owed Pablo an explanation for abandoning his charge to his own devices for an afternoon, and having to kill an American cop would only add to his failings in his boss's eyes. Enio ran a hand over his bald head—the baldness a choice, not the result of a father's faulty genes—before the cop made it to the driver's side window and Enio hit the button to slide the glass between them down.

"Good afternoon, officer," he greeted the cop. He handed the documents through the open window. "To what do I owe this pleasure?"

The cop actually reached up to the brim of his hat and tipped it before he spoke. "Seems to me you might be a little lost, son." He reached for the paperwork. "Thought I'd stop by and see if I could offer assistance."

Enio laughed easily. "I have Waze," he replied, gesturing to the cell phone on the passenger seat.

Still, the cop wanted to know: "Where you goin'?" He leafed through the papers Enio had handed him as he asked.

'Back to Homestead, officer. I am the driver for Mr. David Cohen, the owner of Citizen's National Bank? I am on my way back to his home, in Homestead."

The officer grunted. "You're his chauffeur? Not much of a sense of direction for someone who drives for a living—you need to go south and you're pointed north, son. What were you doin' up here in Coral Gables?"

"Running an errand. For Mr. Cohen."

"Yeah? What errand?"

Enio smiled, thinking he might enjoy killing this man. Thinking, "Just give me a reason…" He said, "Picking up some tickets for a Republican fundraiser."

"Were ya, now?" The cop grunted again, this time adding a little chuckle. "Lemme run these. Be right back."

Enio watched the cop saunter back to his cruiser, his chunky ass wiggling as he walked, big belly leading the way. He was a nosy one, Enio thought, watching again through the sedan's rearview mirror, but hard to tell if he was one of those gringo bigots or just a more benign sort of asshole. The cop stood at the driver's side window of his cruiser, talking into a microphone attached to his dashboard by a curly cord. Enio could hear only the wind from other cars cruising by, a high-pitched parrot voice and intermittent static from the cop's radio; he couldn't make out any words passing between the cop and whoever it was on the other end of the line.

He smiled again as he listened; he really wouldn't mind taking out the cop, but he hoped he wouldn't have to bother. Pablo's wrath aside, cleaning up after the kill would be tricky—it was daylight, the street had a fair flow of traffic, he was driving an easily identifiable car owned by an upright Florida businessman… And he hadn't managed to get rid of even one measly body after a good hour of trying.

The thought of that body—the poor kid decomposing in the trunk—sent a pleasant shudder up

his spine. He felt sorry for the kid, of course—
that kid was no more an assassin than his sainted
mother back in Mexico City—but the dumbass cop
was standing twenty yards away from the dead
body and he had no clue. He was getting his thrill
harassing a brown guy in a nice car. He'd probably shit himself if he knew there was a real crime
to sink his yellow teeth into. Enio tried not to
laugh and glanced again in the rearview. Saw the
cop shake his head and lean into the car to put the
radio mike back into its holder on the dashboard.

"Well, officer?" Enio asked when the cop was
once more at his window.

"Well, son, you're legal."

"That was never a question. As far as I was concerned," Enio replied.

The copy grunted again, handed back the registration and insurance card, Enio's forged driver's
license and concealed carry permit. "Here's a suggestion for you—take this street to the next cross,
take a right and another right and that's going to
put you back on Grenada, and that's going to run
you right into the Dixie Highway. You get on that
going south and you'll get to Homestead, you hear
me?"

"I hear you, officer."

The officer nodded. "So, the great man, David
Cohen's a Republican, is he?" the cop mused.
"He's a Jew, isn't he?" When Enio didn't answer,
the cop added, "Thought most of those people were
libtards." He shrugged at the idea, and turned
back toward his cruiser. He gave the trunk lid a
hearty pat as he passed the end of the car and

called to Enio, "Straight to the next cross street, two rights, Dixie Highway, south."

"Yes, sir. Got it."

"Right," the cop answered. He checked for traffic before he swung open the door and got back into the driver's seat of the cruiser. He sat there for a few seconds, while Enio fired up the engine of the sedan and pulled away. Enio gave his horn a friendly tap as he pulled away from the curb, and the officer returned the farewell with a two-fingered salute out his window.

Chapter 19

My brain felt like it was made of shattered glass. "What the *fuck*?" I muttered, out loud, into the dark all around me. I didn't immediately remember drinking five glasses of straight vodka in rapid succession before passing out—that memory and its accompanying regret would come later —but it wasn't, in any case, the vodka that was causing my most pressing problems. I wasn't breathing properly, for one thing; it was as if I was trying to suck in air through my shirt. And, as I'd woken, I'd rolled my head, and, as my head had rolled over the hard surface on which I was resting, I'd abruptly discovered an exquisitely tender spot at the back of my skull, in the general area behind and a little below my left ear. I reached, automatically, to touch the aching area and I discovered that my hands were bound together, cleverly—diabolically—fastened around my waist so I couldn't get them anywhere near my head. I bent my head to get a look at whatever contraption was binding me—sending a spasm of pain through my neck and right inner ear—and realized the reason I couldn't see was not because the room was dark but because there was a cloth bag wrapped around my head.

I cannot overemphasize the sense of panic that coursed through every fiber in my body. This was not the glorious high of pure adrenaline; this was the human sympathetic nervous system on overdrive, a cocktail of my favored adrenaline mixed with overdoses of cortisol and norepinephrine, now hitting my tissues as if it had been injected by a skilled nurse into a major artery.

My instinct—my first objective—was to calm my heart, which had begun to perform the drum solo from "In-A-Gadda-Da-Vida." If I didn't get my heartbeat under control then the whole muscle was going to explode and no further efforts at discerning the extent of my current predicament, or escaping it, were going to be necessary. I would, simply, die of fright—a form of death that, until that very moment, I would have dismissed as dubious.

It took what I determined was a full ten minutes of breathing alternately between nostrils to get my heart back into the range of standard beats per minute. Breathe in through the right nostril, breathe out through the left... it was a relaxation technique Jack had told me about. His boyfriend had taught it to him and he and I had had a good laugh about how woo-woo it was. I made a mental note to tell Jack that it actually worked—if I lived through whatever mess I was currently in, Jack and I were going to have a hell of a good laugh at ourselves for thinking his boyfriend was so full of shit.

With my heart no longer drumming through my body, drowning out all other sounds from the inside out, I focused on figuring out my physical surroundings. The only senses I had at my immediate disposal were smell, touch, and hearing. The only thing I could smell was the bag over my head, a distinct aroma of coffee cloaking some other scent. Petroleum? Paint? Was it a sack that had been previously used for roasted beans? Was I lying on my back on the floor of a mechanic's garage? I hoped if the latter were true there weren't grease spills on the floor as, I could tell from touch, I was still wearing the dove-gray linen jacket I'd put on that morning, when I had no clue I'd end up somewhere on my ass.

From touch I also easily determined that the cold, hard, concrete upon which I was lying was very smooth, as if it had been polished, or finished with a sealant. That my hands were bound together and to my waist by a relatively thick chain—a chain of greater weight than, I supposed, would have rationally been required to hold me. And that a separate length of chain ran from my wrists to my ankles, which were also bound—together, but on opposite sides of an upright pole. Not a utility pole, something slenderer, and made of metal. A pole dancer's pole, I thought, though more likely some sort of scaffolding. In any case, the manner in which my ankles were fastened to it were going to make it impossible for me to stand, though I supposed I could sit up and, that accomplished, could bow my head and wriggle my hands and find a way to rip the bag off my head.

This, of course, assumed that I was alone in whatever space I was being held. That no one was around who was going to give me another whack on the back of my head and knock me out again.

Which was exactly when I remembered that I had been whacked on the back of the head in the first place.

And by whom.

Francisco?

No, that couldn't be right. Francisco was my bodyguard. There to protect me, not give me a concussion. Yet, the last thing I remembered was nodding off in the front seat of some tiny, tinny car he'd driven to pick me up from Xavier's and, if it hadn't been him, then who?

I groaned as I thought of Xavier. Not because I believed for a minute Xavier had been the one to whack me, because I remembered that Xavier had found me stumbling drunk on the elevator in his building. That my inebriated state had required him to help me out to Francisco's car. To help me into Francisco's care.

Which was not exactly of the tender, loving variety, as far as I could establish, drawing on my admittedly fuzzy memory.

I closed my eyes, breathing shallowly, focusing all my thoughts on my sense of sound and I heard … Nothing.

Not human, not animal, not mechanical. Not even wind moving outside a window, nor traffic going by in the distance. As if I were in some vortex of silence, which fearsome thought shot through my system like another dose of cortisol. When you find yourself suddenly and tightly bound, and blinded by some old coffee bag over your head, it is startlingly easy to drift off in the wonder that maybe you've died and are now experiencing hell.

Inhale through right nostril; exhale through left.

I got my heart rate back to normal range again with formidable concentration. I disallowed myself metaphysical speculation and thought only about what was real. I could breathe, albeit with some difficulty. My ankles were drawn so securely against the metal pole that moving them even a quarter of an inch was agonizing. My head ached, and the back of it throbbed. And I was thirsty.

I was so very thirsty.

These pains were proof enough, in the moment, that I was actually alive.

I gathered my courage and some precious spit on my arid tongue and I squeaked, "Hello?"

I waited for an answer that didn't come.

So I tried again, louder this time. "Hello?"

Again I waited and, again, still nothing.

So I screamed at the top of my lungs, "*Hello! Hell to the fucking hello! Is anybody out there*?" and all I accomplished was to make those shards of glass that were the current composition of my brain rattle around and lacerate whatever organic matter was left inside my vodka-soaked skull.

Chapter 20

Iт was late—dark—by the time Enio returned to Clint's condo. He was exhausted, but filled with the pride of the soldier he used to be: his day had been purposeful. The disposal of the body, while it had frustrated him for hours, had been accomplished and, at the end, with relative ease. He'd followed the cop's orders—like many people who'd grown up in the religious traditions of Catholicism, he clung to certain superstitions and found something providential in the cop's directions; he'd pointed himself north on the Dixie Highway. Outside of a town called Hallandale Beach he noticed a marina that had seen better days and pulled into the structure's one-story, cement-block parking garage.

The garage was dark and as ill-maintained as the marina seemed to be—only a few bulbs remained burning in the garage's fixtures as well as atop the battered, lantern-shaped lights on poles driven into the dock at every seventh or eighth piling. He backed the sedan into a space near to the land heads, where the dock began its stretch into the water, and got out to have a look around.

There were few boats in the slips—only about half of them with a tenant—mostly power boats, several weather-beaten fishing boats, half a dozen sad houseboats, a couple of crappy pontoon boats, one scruffy but ancient cigarette boat. Two small sailboats, one left to the elements and the other shrouded in canvas. He spotted an old hound at the far end of the dock, and the dog spotted him too, but long enough only to lift his head, have a sniff at the air, and return to its nap. The only human life he encountered was what he inferred from the light of a small television set coming from inside one of the houseboats.

He moved quietly to the end of the dock, past the hound who was either too old or too bored to acknowledge him, and into the cockpit of the least-decrepit specimen he could find—a white-and-red cuddy cabin craft. He slipped a folding knife from an inside pocket of his jacket, knelt under the steering wheel, and, when the boat was efficiently hot-wired, it roared to life.

"Jesus," he whispered, as the sound echoed off the water. Still on his knees, he kept alert for any sign of discovery. The marina, however, remained serene as the motor sputtered into a soft hum. He checked the fuel tank, gratified that the boat he'd chosen was filled with more than enough gas to get him where he needed to go, and back again, and then cut the engine to go retrieve his cargo. Three rickety dock carts were lined up against a wall of the dock shop. He used his knife to slice through the nylon rope binding one of them to an old bicycle rack and wheeled it toward the parking garage.

He looked around the garage before he popped the trunk, scanning for surveillance cameras and, given the general shabbiness of the place, was not surprised that none had been installed. "OK, kid, let's go," he whispered as he pulled the body from the trunk. The tarp around the body had remained tightly wrapped, and the man had been on the smallish side to begin with, so Enio didn't even break a sweat loading him into the cart and wheeling him, as well as two associated trash bags, out to the boat.

The body lay in the cockpit, at Enio's feet as he piloted the boat through the Straits of Florida, toward the Atlantic. He spoke to it as they bumped through the water. "You know, I don't even know your name." He rubbed his hand over his head, feeling the stubble that had grown over the course of the day, looking forward to shaving it clean in the shower later. "You would have thought Charlotte would have mentioned your name. Grieved your passing in some way. You worked together, after all." He looked to the sky, the starry night. "Something wrong with that girl, maybe?" He shrugged; whether there was or not, it was none of his concern. "I will call you my amigo, and tell you I am sorry you had to die." He shook his head. "I think you did not have to, really." Yes, he thought, that was more accurate. The young man at his feet was not a killer; he had merely gotten in the way of the real assassin. His death was a waste.

And waste angered Enio.

He raised his head and let the salty, ocean wind blow over his face.

"I think," Enio addressed the body again, "you were too young to have a wife. But maybe you left a sweetheart behind? And a mother. Did you have a living mother, amigo?" He piloted the boat in silence for several minutes. "I think you are like me, Catholic, and your mother would like it if I pray for you."

And so he did. He prayed while he drove the boat. And while the boat idled in choppy Atlantic waters. While he crawled to the front of the boat and opened the hatch that held the anchor, and cut the anchor and a good length of its rope loose, and wrapped the rope around the body, as well as the associated trash bags, and tied it off. While he threw his amigo overboard, into the welcoming deep.

Enio dumped his armful of VHS tapes onto the overstuffed chair in Clint's living room.

"What do you have there?" Jack asked.

"Three weeks of security tapes from the desk downstairs," Enio said, and eyed the half-eaten pizza on the coffee table in front of Charlotte and Jack.

"Have a slice," Charlotte told him. "And we re-stocked the beer too—grab one out of the fridge."

"One slice," Enio said, reaching into the box. "And the beer when I get back. I just have to pick up Mr. Kennedy. Where is Francisco?"

Charlotte tilted her head, and Jack squinted at him. "Francisco went to pick up Clint," he said.

Enio dropped the pizza back in its box. "When? When did Francisco go?"

Charlotte put her own slice down on her plate, resting on the table. "He went a couple hours ago."

"And where did he go?" Enio demanded. *"How did he know where to go?"*

Jack finished chewing, and swallowed so he could answer, "He called Clint, I guess. He got his number from my phone."

Enio rubbed his head. He had wanted a shower and a shave so very much.

Charlotte cleared her throat. "Enio, tell us what's wrong."

Enio shook his head. "I don't know," he said. "I don't yet know."

Chapter 21

I screamed until my voice was hoarse. Until my head felt as if the shattered glass inside of it was going to rip it open. Until I grew faint from breathing in all the carbon dioxide I was breathing out and into the bag over my head. Until it was impossible to scream because I was so dehydrated it felt as if my tongue was a clump of kitty litter.

I lay, panting, on the concrete floor and thought: so, this is how it ends.

And then I thought: *Fuck that.*

But I knew immediately and instinctively that escape—freedom—was too large a goal to set. That my thinking would become unfocused if I was trying to plan two and five and ten steps ahead, especially before I understood the whole of what I was dealing with. Seeing the big picture had always been one of my gifts, and at the moment I couldn't see a goddamned thing. What I had to do was to concentrate my efforts on each small step along the way and that meant the first order of business was going to have to be to get the fucking bag off my head.

I took a deep breath and pulled myself into an upright, seated position. I kept myself in good shape, so the sit-up wasn't difficult, though the pain the effort caused in my already aching brain made me woozy, and I still half expected that showing any definitive sign of life was going to cause someone to bring something hard down on my head and knock me out again.

I waited a moment for the blow and, when none came, I lifted my hands and bowed my head as far as I was able. The fact that my hands were encumbered by the chain around my waist and my feet were still tethered to the metal pole was a bit of a problem—my hamstrings had always been tighter than optimal—but I managed to bring the tips of my fingers to my neck and feel the cord that was wrapped around it to hold the bag in place. The cord felt fuzzy, like fleece or a heavy flannel—like the belt of a bathrobe; my fingers fumbled to find the knot which, I realized after several panicky minutes, must have been tied behind my head.

I allowed myself a break at that point, to sit up straight and stretch the muscles in my back, and to calm my respiration once again. I had to keep the reality that my air supply was limited top-of-mind; if I sucked all the available oxygen out of my bag before the carbon dioxide had time to dissipate through the fibers, all I'd accomplish was to make myself pass out. When I felt level-headed again, I bowed once more and began the slow and arduous task of easing that cord around my neck a millimeter or two at a time to find the knot.

I slipped into an almost meditative state while I worked. I could not afford the thought that, at any moment, my captor could return to that room, jerk the bag back into place and destroy any progress I'd made, so my mantra became *small steps, small steps, small steps* and, in this frame of mind, every millimeter I managed to turn that cord became a victory.

By the time my fingers touched on the knot, the muscles in my back had stretched enough that I could reach more of my hands to my neck to manipulate the cord. I allowed myself a sigh of celebration and began to work my fingers inside the loops of the knots—yes, *knots*; plural. I knew as soon as I touched the bulk that the cord had been double tied. I almost choked myself in my first attempt to yank an end through and loose; so, after I was done coughing and gasping for air that wasn't available, I changed my mantra to *patience, patience, patience* and worked the cord even more slowly and deliberately until I was able to pull the first, and then the second knot free.

I rolled my head freely from shoulder to shoulder. The motion exacerbated my headache, but it made my neck feel wonderful. I hadn't realized how tightly the cord had been tied until it was gone. The motion, however, did nothing to dislodge the bag on my head and I had to duck my head lower and stretch my back muscles to their absolute limit until I was able to get the top of the bag between my two middle fingers and yank it off.

I pulled air into my lungs like... Well, like the dying man I suppose I had been. One cannot live without air, of course, and I vowed I would never again take breathing for granted. I allowed myself three, good, deep breaths and then I started to look around. The first place I looked was at my wrists, because they were sore, and I saw that they were bleeding, both of them, where pulling against the chain had chaffed the skin off the end of my bony radius. Bloody streaks were smeared all over the sleeves and midsection of my dove-gray sport coat, mingling there with the few spatters of Charlotte's dried blood, and it was a measure of the urgency of my situation that, in the moment, it didn't occur to me to grieve for that favorite, expensive article of clothing.

I was, indeed, in a garage—a two-car garage, neat as could be, sparkling, freshly painted, white shelves with nothing on them lining the far wall, a pristine and polished, newly poured concrete floor, hook-ups for washer/dryer in a small niche by a door that, in any standard layout, led to the house's kitchen. I was in a new build, a house that had just gone up and was still being prepared to go on the market, and my bet was that, when I got outside, I'd see that it was located in a new development—a good choice on the part of my kidnappers, as I could scream as loudly as I actually had and no one would hear me. There was a window on the wall opposite the kitchen door and through it I could see that it was dark outside—night. The only signs that other humans had at one point been in this garage with me were an ashtray filled with stinking butts in a corner nearest to the garage door and, next to it, two plastic bottles of Coca-Cola. One of the bottles was empty, and on its side, and the other was half-full, capped, as if its owner wanted to preserve the carbonation until he came back later to finish the drink. The idea that someone might be returning for the rest of that soda goosed my sense of urgency.

Still, I was—quite literally—dying of thirst. Coca-Cola, as it happened, was my go-to hangover comfort, and I took it as some sort of sign from providence that a bottle of it had been provided to me. I had to get to that Coke. The small step I would have to take, before I could take the step of rehydrating my arid body, was to become ambulatory. To get my feet loose. I glanced down at them, chained on either side of scaffolding pipe, still shod in the tan Ferragamo loafers I'd put on that morning, when I'd still been a free man, and I laughed out loud at what I saw. My kidnapper —or kidnappers; who was to say there was only one?—was one stupid fuck: he'd left my shoes on when he tied me up. I slipped my right foot out of the loafer and began to wiggle it through the loop of the chain until it was free, at which point the figure eight the chain had made between my legs collapsed and I was able to pull it around the pole, stand up and walk freely.

My arms were cinched to my waist, a length of chain dangling from them, and I gathered it up so it wouldn't trip me as I stumbled to the divine bottle of Coke. I got down on my knees before the elixir and bent from the waist until I could get it between my hands to uncap it and, then, as if it was a body memory and not at all an intellectual understanding that I wouldn't be able to use my hands to bring it to my mouth, I set it back on the concrete and leaned over, wrapped my lips around the top, gripped the grooves with my teeth, and lifted it in the air until the blessed liquid spilled into my hungry mouth.

It fizzled and I gulped, and I didn't spill a drop.

When the bottle was empty, I spit it out. I was panting again, but I was also feeling like a new man. *Small steps*, I reminded myself; *don't get cocky.* I jogged back to the pole and slipped my one bare foot back into my loafer—wherever I was going to go from this point I was going to have to go on foot and better not try to do it in stocking feet. I scanned the garage, then trotted over to the door that I assumed led into the house, wriggled a hand to grasp the handle and found that it was locked. *Fuck*, I muttered, though my attention had already turned to the garage door on the other wall. I saw the button that would open it to its left. I trotted over to the button, the length of chain that had once been bound around my feet still gathered in my hands, said a prayer that the door was operational, and—because it had been installed at about shoulder height—hit the button with my nose.

Chapter 22

XAVIER put a finger above the knot in his tie and yanked it loose. He'd rarely felt choked by the uniform he put on every morning—the suit and tie and wingtips—but he'd put in a full day already; now it was night and he still had a good hour to go until it was over. Why was the guy voted Top Attorney in Miami for nine out of the last ten years still putting in sixteen-hour days? He had associates for that.

He also had—this made him both smile and sigh—a fair number of clients who were more than clients, who were friends; and it was his own perfectionist compulsions that compelled him to work overtime for them. The Cohens would just have to deal with his loosened tie. He smiled more broadly, as if his after-hours casual would throw those lovely people. David was probably already in their kitchen, where they would gather for this meeting, and Candace was likely already preparing a pitcher of Manhattans in anticipation of his arrival.

Traffic was light and the drive was easy. And that Manhattan was going to taste awfully good.

"Have you talked to Clint?" Enio demanded.

"Well, no. Not personally. Francisco talked to him—" Jack offered.

"Fuck," Enio replied, yanking his phone out of his jacket pocket and punching in Clint's number, pacing as it rang—and rang—and went to voice mail. "Fuck," he repeated. He was angry, though mostly at himself; he had let his guard down and that little punk had gotten it over on him. Yes, he had been suspicious of Francisco for some time— or, more truthfully, he hadn't liked him from the first, had tried to warn Pablo of his misgivings, had privately accused the old man of slipping because he would not take those warnings seriously and, even so, he had underestimated his opponent and been had. Both his training and his temperament had failed him and he needed to make it right.

Charlotte leaned over and took his hand in hers. "I wish you would tell us what's going on."

I would if I knew, Enio thought. He shook off her grip and said, "The last place I took Clint, to Xavier Sousa's restaurant. Can you be in touch with this Xavier Sousa?"

"Yeah." Jack jumped to, sprinting into the kitchen. "I have his number in my cell—it's just in here charging—"

Enio waited for what he knew was coming.

"Where the fuck is my phone?" Jack called, as if either Charlotte or Enio could put hands on it.

"Francisco has it," Enio told them.

"Why would Francisco..." Jack wondered, refusing to allow the truth to dawn.

"Can you look up Xavier Sousa's phone number, please," Enio asked him.

"I— It's a private number. Unlisted."

"Right," Enio said.

The sound of thinking was like thunder in the room.

"Hold on!" Jack waggled his fingers at Enio. "Give me your phone. Of course I know my parents' number. They'll have Xavier's."

Francisco sat with his colleague, Henri, in a back booth of a darkened bar in Little Havana—The Latin Kitchen, it billed itself. "They're going to start calling around," Henri said, as Francisco silenced Clint's cell. "They are starting to find out their friend is missing. You must not lose your nerve now."

Henri was a sixty-one-year old man with a pronounced French accent who bragged about having lived illegally in Miami since the late 1980s. "I am good-looking, and I have a charming accent," he'd say, and laugh when he proclaimed that he was an illegal immigrant. "And I am white. Everyone looks right by me when they think of aliens!"

Henri was growing less good-looking, however, with each passing year, though his job transporting goods from Nuevo León, for Francisco's boss, Mateo, was steady and long-term. Or, it was steady when he was sober, which, like his looks, was a fading attribute.

"I should have just killed him, like Mateo wants," Francisco said, and he picked up the mug of beer that was in front of him and drained it.

Henri shrugged. "You will still kill him. But, oh, my young friend, if you kill him too quickly, you will be missing out on a great opportunity. This Clint Kennedy, who is now in your custody? He is the son of a very rich man—"

"He's not his son."

"Some say so, others not so." Henri gave another exaggerated, Gallic shrug. "The truth does not matter as this very rich man loves your Clint Kennedy as if it is so and he will pay us to keep him alive. When he has paid us, then we make the son dead, like Mateo says."

Francisco threw the wad of paper he'd made of Clint's list across the table at Henri. "Look again at the nice red circle around Mateo's name on that paper. He knows who wants him dead, and who else has he told this to? Pablo? Has he told this to Pablo?"

Henri shook his head. "You are worried about the wrong things," he said. "Mateo wants Pablo's little pet dead only to prove a point. Pablo won't start a war to protect his puppy—he'll be happy enough that no one is any longer shooting at him. You'll see. Now!" Henri clapped his hands together. "Garcon! Another round for us here, merci d'avance!"

"Mom?" Jack said when Candace picked up.

"Jack?"

"Yeah, Mom—"

"Why are you calling from a blocked number?"

"Oh, ah, it's a friend's phone. I've misplaced mine."

"Well, that was careless of you."

"Yes, I know, look, hey, is Clint with you?"

Enio threw up his arms and Jack waved a hand at him and looked away, mouthing, "At least I should ask..."

"No, dear, he's not." Candace paused. "Is he supposed to be?"

Jack closed his eyes. "Not necessarily. So, Mom, I need Xavier's cell number. Will you give it to me, please?"

"Of course. Let me go look it up," she said and put the phone down. The elder Cohens both had cell phones—it was 2009, after all—but Candace still wasn't used to looking up phone numbers on hers. She still relied on a paper system, the mid-sized, leather-bound black book she kept on her desk in the little room off the kitchen she used as an office. Jack thought it would be faster to just let her go get the black book rather than try once again, in the moment, to teach her how to use her phone's search feature.

"What?" Enio snapped as Jack paced.

Jack held up a finger. "She's getting it. Yeah, Mom?"

"Yes, sweetie. His number is 555-8791 but, you know what? He's on his way here."

"Xavier is?"

"Yes, he's bringing the paperwork for me to sign, so I can become Elmer Collier's guardian until Clint works out his little problem with that nasty woman at the elder care facility. Why don't you come over and you can have a drink with us? We'll have a nice—"

"On the way, Mom."

Xavier pulled into the Cohens' circular drive, parked his car and took a moment to stretch his back. His wife had suggested he buy one of those lumbar-support pillows if driving was beginning to bother him so much and he thought—not for the first time—that she'd had a good idea. He made a mental note to go online and look for one when he got home and hoped he wouldn't forget to do it again.

In any case, the drive was going to be easier going home. He'd be more relaxed. Not because he was going to drink so much—he was, after all, driving, so he'd have just one of Candace's exceptional Manhattans, nurse that until she offered him coffee to end the evening, as Candace always did. It was the company that was going to loosen him up. Maybe he wouldn't even bring up Clint in the course of the evening. Yes, Clint had been in disgusting shape when he'd seen him at his building this afternoon, but the guy had just been through an ordeal. Xavier supposed that anyone who'd recently endured a police interrogation—for murder, no less, even if it had been a casual questioning—deserved to blow off some steam. It wasn't up to him to report Clint to the Cohens for every infraction, certainly—tattle to the parents about an errant son.

No. Tonight he'd make sure the guardianship business was taken care of, then spend the rest of the evening unwinding in pleasant company. Being able to tell Clint in the morning that he no longer had to worry about Elmer Collier would do wonders to relieve some of his stress.

Xavier stretched one more time, pulled off his tie completely, hung it on the rearview mirror, and climbed out of his car. He reached for his cell phone, sitting in the console, but on second thought left it where it sat. He was calling it: his work day was officially over. If anyone needed him, they could call his office in the morning. It was a balmy night, so he ditched his suit jacket as well, draping it over the driver's seat lest it wrinkle, grabbed his briefcase and headed toward the front door.

"Candace? David?" he called after ringing the bell, because the front door was standing open.

"In the kitchen, Xavier. Come on back," David called in return.

"On my way," Xavier replied.

Chapter 23

THE sound of that garage door rising, the motor humming low and the whirr of the metal as the door rolled up into the ceiling, was like listening to The Vienna Boys' Choir in the midst of a song of jubilant praise. I looked into the darkness outside —the starry sky, the not-yet-paved, empty street lined with American Dream houses under construction—and I slipped out into the silent night.

I ran for about a quarter of a mile—no small feat when you're trying to stay inconspicuous, in the shadows, and your wrists are chained to your waist—until I had left the construction zone behind and was in an adjoining residential area that was actually populated. There was a large palm tree in the side yard of a small, yellow bungalow, and I ducked behind it. The first thing I did was shimmy my upper body around so I could get my upper arm as close as possible to the inside pocket of my jacket, where I typically carried my phone, just to make sure it wasn't there. It was gone, of course—I'd already tried checking that pocket several other times, and what self-respecting kidnapper was going to leave a phone in such easy reach of his victim?—and I finally put the idea of an easy rescue to rest. I really was going to have to do this on foot.

I tentatively stepped out from behind the tree, trying to get my bearings. From the look of the houses, I could have been in any middle-income suburb of any American city, though the palm trees in the front yards narrowed down the geography considerably. "Good God," I thought, and stepped behind the shadow of the large palm tree again. There were lights on in the bungalow behind it, and I saw motion through the window— a man sitting down in front of a television set, a can of something, beer or soda, in his hand. He looked to his left and I saw his mouth move, talking to someone else in there who I couldn't see. I had a wild impulse to run to the door of that yellow bungalow and bang on it as hard as I could, pleading for help, but the certainty that the occupants would take one look at me—chained, with blood smeared all over my jacket—and slam the door in my face before calling the police stayed the impulse. That was one more bit of drama I could easily do without.

Still, I wondered, what was so wrong with the police getting involved? I'd been *kidnapped*, shouldn't I *want* someone to call the police? I felt righteous for all of five seconds before I realized that the police would probably ask me if I knew who my kidnapper was and I had a nasty suspicion about that. While I wouldn't crack and tell them outright—Francisco! It was Francisco!—there was a decent chance they would discover in the course of the investigation they would inevitably launch that the culprit was the man charged with being my bodyguard by the South American drug kingpin with whom I was in business.

Yeah, no. Not a good look. Not going to get the police involved.

Still, standing out in the open air about a quarter mile from where my kidnapper had dumped me and dealing with the expectation that, sooner rather than later, he'd return, find out I was missing and start looking for me, was not a soothing consideration. I had to do *something*.

That was when providence gave me my next big break. The man in the yellow bungalow got up and threw open the window. I shrank back into the shadow of the palm tree while I watched him go from window to window in the house and throw them all open to the sweet night air. The man was probably my age, maybe a few years older, wearing a wifebeater over a fine torso, and I heard him say to the person who was in the room with him, "*Ven, a levantarte, vamous a bailar!*" Then I heard the music. The Buena Vista Social Club. I was pleased to see his companion rise, a young woman who may or may not have been beautiful, but she swung her hips like the very definition of temptation. I was pleased because the music made me want to dance too. There would be dancing all over the globe, and world peace, if only more people would listen to the Buena Vista Social Club. I knew immediately I was in the Grove, the section that had, in my time, been the Irish ghetto but was now a haven for Cuban immigrants.

And that meant that the house Charlotte Cruet shared with her father, Chester—Cuban immigrant via the 1980 Mariel boatlift—was not far. But how far? Which direction to start jogging? I had no idea. I allowed myself another break here, watching the man in the wifebeater and the woman with the swiveling hips whirl the whole way through "Chan Chan." Then I put my finger to the wind and set out.

Chapter 24

Xavier accepted Candace's delicious Manhattan —rocks, served in a crystal tumbler so heavy you could have used it for a weapon—and his first sip felt like relief itself. Even his aching lumbar region seemed to relax. "Candace," he said, "you should have been a bartender. You missed your calling."

"Don't I know it!" David agreed, sipping his own cocktail—a small sip, nursing the half portion Candace allowed him; she had become rather strict with his allotment of alcohol since his stroke and, as in all things, he bowed to her wishes and made do.

"Business first," Xavier decreed. He took another sip of his drink then put it down on the marble counter and produced the guardianship request from his briefcase. "Read it over, and then sign here," he told her, indicating the yellow stick-it note his secretary had attached to the document. "Clint hasn't signed yet, but I'll call him in the morning and we'll take care of that."

"You think you'll have any trouble, getting the judge to sign off on it?" David asked.

Xavier made a pffft sound. "Legally, it's no problem. Clint was what they call the 'pre-need' guardian and, with that, it's his option to appoint another Florida resident in his place. And as for Kushner? He'll be happy to have it off his desk. Just among the three of us, I don't think Kushner's long for the bench."

"Why is that?" Candace asked, more of a polite inquiry than an indication of any real interest.

Xavier shook his head. "He's been... How shall I put it? A bit unreliable in the last few months. Making any number of little, foolish mistakes, like this one about Elmer Collier. A few of his friends and I... we've had some casual conversations with him about retirement and I'm hoping he comes around to seeing that's the best thing."

David fished the maraschino cherry out of his glass. "Well, if you have any trouble with him on this, let me know. I can give him a call."

Xavier nodded. There was no need for further questions. Both he and David had deep roots in the community, a series of ties that bound them within the web of people who ran the city, the state, and beyond. No need to ask what courtesy David had extended to Judge Kushner—what David might hold over his head. It was enough to know there was a favor owed and David was willing to call it in for the cause. Xavier said, "This is really kind of you, Candace, to take responsibility for Elmer Collier. You don't have to do this, of course."

"Of course, I do," Candace replied, taking the Mont Blanc pen Xavier offered her and adding her elegant signature to the document. "This is exactly the sort of thing you do for the children, after all." She folded the document and handed it to Xavier. "Well, now that it's official, I suppose I'd better go and pay Elmer a visit."

Xavier put the papers back into his briefcase. "That's not absolutely necessary, Candace. You know Elmer isn't responsive, right? He really has no idea what's going on around him—"

"Are you sure of that, Xavier?"

"Well—"

"The only thing that scares me about getting older is ending up in a nursing home, my body having given out but my mind intact." She lifted her glass to Xavier's. He returned the gesture and they clinked the crystal. "I think I'll go read to him … I wonder if he might enjoy *The Help*? It's this month's selection for my book club."

"Shouldn't we call somebody? You know, tell them we have Clint Kennedy and we want the money for him?" Francisco had finished his third beer, all IPAs that Henri recommended, as well as nearly an entire vial of Henri's superior cocaine, and all that stimulation was making him feel more confident about the enterprise.

"Not yet," Henri advised. "We need to give them a little time to panic. The more upset they are when they hear from us, the more leverage we have. Besides"—he motioned to the waiter for another round—"have you even thought about how much money we're going to ask for?"

The blank look on Francisco's face was the admission that he had not. "A hundred thousand dollars?"

Henri scoffed. "Vous pensez petit!" he exclaimed. "The Cohens, these are rich people, boy. What is a hundred thousand dollars to them? Why not a million dollars? Hmmm? What do you think of that? Do you think your Clint Kennedy is worth a million dollars?"

It occurred to Francisco that Mateo wasn't paying him one extra peso to take out Kennedy—the prisoner was worth much more to him alive than dead. At least for the time being. He could kill him after they'd counted the money. "Why not a million?"

"Half for you, and half for me!" Henri smiled. "And, tell me, what will you do with your half?"

Francisco waited to reply until the waiter had served them their fresh beers and left the table. Then he giggled. "What would I not do with half a million dollars?" he asked.

"Why are we driving to Homestead?" Enio could have smacked Jack in his pretty face. "It is half an hour to Homestead, forty minutes, even if we go fast—do you think we have all the time in the world? Call this number! Call your friend, Xavier!"

"Xavier is at my parents' house!" Jack shouted back at him. "If Clint's really in trouble, that's not something I want to tell my parents over the phone —especially my mom."

"Mierda! You stupid man! You would rather tell your mother he's dead?"

That put Jack back on his heels. Charlotte too. "You think... he's in that much danger?" she asked.

"The bullet that I dug out of your arm today? That was meant for him! Is that enough danger for you?"

Charlotte nodded, her fingers to her mouth, stifling a gasp. "Jack, call Xavier. Please. Call Xavier right now."

Chapter 25

It took me a couple of turns around the neighborhood to get my bearings and figure out the direction I had to head in to hit the Cruet house, ducking behind fences and crouching from shrub to shrub. But once I knew where I had to go, I threw caution to the wind, broke into a flat-out run, sprinting to my destination.

I was almost running on empty by the time I spotted the little bungalow Charlotte shared with her father, and I choked on a gasp of air when I saw the whole place was dark and realized no one was home. I beat it around to the back of the house and sank into one of the woven nylon folding chairs that sat on the Cruets' tiny patio. I wanted to cry—wanted so desperately to be rescued, to have this nightmare come to an end—and it took me a few minutes to decide not to. I was safe here, after all—right? I was in friendly territory, a place where Francisco wouldn't know to come looking for me. And the door that led into the Cruets' kitchen was one of those back doors that had a solid wooden bottom and a top made up of six glass panes—three stacked on top of three.

The door was locked, as I knew it would be when I tried it, but all I had to do was break the pane of glass nearest the handle and reach inside and I could let myself in.

Or, I could have done this if my hands weren't chained to my waist.

I had no Plan B, but Plan A was going to require a few modifications.

I looked around the yard. It was tidy and unremarkable, a miniscule plot of fairly green, clipped grass, broken up by that postage stamp patio furnished with two old-fashioned folding lawn chairs and a small, three-legged, faux-wood table, made of some plastic compound that had been molded to resemble the bark of a tree. There were no rocks, no garden tools, no flower pot I could pick up and heave through the pane of glass I was desperate to break.

But.

Wait.

I dropped the length of chain I'd been carrying —the length that had been used to secure my feet —and bent to pick up the table. It was heavier than I'd expected it to be, and cumbersome to lift because I couldn't separate my hands to get a firm grip on either side of it, but I got it in the air and aimed one of the legs at the pane of glass.

My first blow and the table slipped out of my hands, bounced once on the concrete step at the back door and landed on its side. It just wasn't possible to keep a grip on it and approach the glass from the angle I'd been shooting for, trying to bring the leg down on the pane. I dropped to my knees to maneuver the table back up on its legs, used the table to balance myself to stand back up, and picked it up again. This time, when I lifted the table, I rested one of the legs directly on the glass, and then I drew it toward me again, only about an inch, and rammed it into the glass.

The shattering sound was, in that moment, better music to my ears than anything the Buena Vista Social Club had ever recorded. I poked out a few shards of glass that remained at the bottom of the pane, tossed the table aside and tried to reach in to unlock the door.

Let's just say that my grasp exceeded my reach —I knew what I had to do to get inside, but with a wingspan of about three-quarters of an inch, there was no way to get my hand far enough inside the door to turn the knob. I had another moment of despair—those seemed to be coming at me fast and furiously—and I flailed my bound hands hard and moaned like a fucking cow until the intense pain in my wrists slowed me down. There was fresh blood dripping down the front of my jacket. I swallowed hard, closed my eyes and concentrated on my breathing again to slow down my whole body, which was shaking with impotent rage.

"Hold on a minute, buddy," I whispered to myself —a demented little pep talk, but talking to myself calmed me down enough to think clearly again. "What if you could wiggle the chain up your torso? That could give you enough leeway to bend at the waist and reach enough of your arm and shoulder in through the broken pane to get a grip on the knob."

My captors had fastened that chain tight, but I pulled up with my hands and used my elbows to roll the chain upward and sucked in my abs until I got that son of a bitch nearly up to my pecs. I could no longer take more than the shallowest of breaths, but I got my hands on that fucking doorknob.

I had to step quickly when the door swung open—my shoulder was still inside the pane, and the dangling length of chain had wrapped itself around my legs—and I took a moment to stand still before I wriggled my shoulder free, kicked the chain to untangle it, and reeled it back up into my grasp. The kitchen was dark and I ran my right arm along the wall closest to the door, where I thought a normal home would have a light switch, found it and flicked it on with my shoulder. It took a second for my eyes to adjust to the light—and my heart a few beats to process Charlotte's scent of fresh-cut pine that lingered in the room—and then I scanned the room for a phone. Chester was an old guy; I was sure he still had a landline.

Did he ever. There, on the opposite wall, near the stove, at about eye level, was a harvest-gold wall model with a dirty, tangled, fifteen-foot cord and fucking rotary dial.

I took a deep breath and then I walked over to the artifact, determined to rescue myself.

My first hurdle was to get the receiver off the hook. This I accomplished by gripping it carefully between my chin and my shoulder, and then bending slowly and, ever so tenderly, depositing it on stovetop. I listened for a second before I stood up, to assure myself the relic had a dial tone.

I knew exactly who I was going to call. Not Xavier—he'd have too many questions—and not the Cohens because I was sure Candace would answer and how the hell would I explain my predicament to her in a way that didn't scare the fuck out of her? Jack. That was who I wanted on the other end of the line. I squared my shoulders to get myself through this next—maybe last?—hurdle.

I thought about dialing the phone with my tongue—that would have been the simplest solution—but when I tried, I quickly discovered that the tongue is a muscle not designed for that much sustained contraction. The masseter muscle on the right side of my face cramped so powerfully I actually squeaked with pain.

"OK, next," I said when I could speak again.

I needed an object with which to turn the dial— a pencil came immediately to mind—but I didn't spot any sort of writing utensil in a quick scan of the kitchen. There were drawers lining the work area, however, that were waist high and I went from one to the other, flinging them open and rummaging through them as quickly as I could until I found—a chopstick.

That would have to do.

I bent to pick it up with my teeth and returned to the phone and realized as soon as I tried to dial the first number that it was too long to efficiently do the job. I spit it out carefully onto the stove top, near my hands so I could pick it up and break it in half, then I bent to get the thicker half in my teeth again. If anyone ever asks, yes, half a chopstick in your mouth and you can dial a rotary phone like a pro. I listened to it ring and didn't wait for a "hello" before I leaned over the receiver on the stove and started screaming into the receiver.

"Jack, listen, you've got to come to Charlotte's house immediately, or faster, I've been kidnapped, I managed to get away and I got myself to Charlotte's house, just get in the car and come and get me right now, I can't go anywhere, my hands are tied and I swear to you this isn't a joke, Jack, are you listening—"

It occurred to me he should have been saying something in response.

"Jack?"

"And just where is Charlotte's house," I heard a man ask in a cheesy French accent.

Chapter 26

"Now," said Henri. "Now would be the time to call the Cohens."

"Fuck that," Francisco shouted, causing the other patrons of The Latin Kitchen to look toward their table with varying degrees of alarm. Francisco lowered his voice but spoke no less emphatically: "Fuck that, Henri, now is the time to go find that little motherfucker and kill him like I wanted to do when I first got my hands on him. You know what Mateo's going to do to me if he's not dead by the time I leave Miami? You think I'm going to have another chance to get close to him and do it once he makes his way back to Enio?"

Henri sat back in his chair. "I wonder how he got away…"

"Does that matter? Does it matter!"

"No, but I'd be curious to find out—"

"Jesus Christ, Henri! If Mateo finds out what we tried to pull, we're both dead!"

"Both of us? Not me, ami. What have I done?"

"Motherfucker! You convinced me to hold that gringo for ransom—"

Henri make a tut-tutting sound with his teeth. "This would be your word against mine. Comprendre, I have worked honorably for Mateo for many decades. You? You are just a boy who has proved nothing—"

"Motherfucker!" Francisco was shouting again, attracting attention.

"Shh, shh, shh," Henri soothed. "If you are so upset, then I think you should follow my plan. It is not too late, I think, for us to get our money. Your captive, he cannot have gotten far. Did you hear him say he still had the chain around his hands? He's probably still in Little Havana. You and I will get in the car and we'll go find him, bring him back to us. Meantime, we call the Cohens, so they can start to get our money out of their bank. Don't you want half a million dollars for yourself? All that nice, hard cash? Don't you want it?"

Francisco seemed to calm considerably as Henri talked. When Henri stopped talking, Francisco gave him his answer: "What I want is you dead," he said, and pulled the Glock from his shoulder holster and shot him in the neck.

Francisco seemed surprised at himself. A little in awe that Henri's blood had spattered so far, left an abstract design on Francisco's own neck, and made his linen jacket quite damp. There hadn't been a loud bang when the gun when off—it was equipped with a silencer, of course—but still the other patrons in the bar caught on to what had happened rather quickly and Francisco heard them gasp and scream and duck behind tables, so he whirled on them. "Anyone of you says one word, tries to stop me, I'll shoot this whole fucking place and everyone in it to hell!"

The crowd grew instantaneously still, remained dutifully silent, and parted for him as he ran out to the parking lot, got in his little rental car, and squealed into traffic.

"Still no answer," Charlotte said from the back-seat. "Obviously Xavier is unable"—she paused —"or unwilling to answer his phone. Maybe his phone's dead, you know. Do you want me to keep trying?"

Jack was certain he wanted her to do that. Mostly because he wasn't at all sure what else there was to do except sit here, in the passenger seat of his father's car, while Enio drove like a fucking lunatic, a minimum of fifteen miles over the limit, speeding to his parents' house. The limbo of being in this car, while unanswered questions swirled through the night, was killing him —and, he could tell from the clenched muscles in Enio's neck and jaw, it was enraging Enio. As if it was physically painful that he had no control over what was happening. "Yes!" Jack wanted to shout at Charlotte, "keep calling until he damned well picks up!" but he was afraid to speak. To not defer to Enio.

"Go ahead," Enio said. "Ring him one more time."

Jack bowed his head at the words, grateful for them, for Enio not giving up on the one thing they were able to do while they sped to his mom and dad's house.

"Shit," Charlotte said, "where's your charger, Enio? Your phone just died."

"Oh, for the love of God, Charlotte." Jack swiveled to face the back seat and snapped at her, "Use your phone!"

Chester Cruet. This was the name that came up on Jack's cell phone. Francisco held it to catch the light from a streetlamp as he passed under it, then checked the rearview mirror again. So far, no one at all was following him. It was as if he'd just left a fantasy, a murder he had only dreamed of and not actually done. Sooner or later, however, one of those assholes at the bar was going to call the police about the dead guy at the back table, and probably give the cops a description of his rental car. It pissed him off that he'd have to ditch the Mitsubishi; that he'd have to go to that trouble. At the next streetlamp he scrolled quickly through Jack's contacts, which included the phone number for Charlotte Cruet, but no address. Fuck it, he thought, it wasn't going to do anybody any good if the police caught up with him before he could catch up with Clint Kennedy, so he turned the car into a small parking lot abutting a convenience store to find himself a new set of wheels.

"No, really"—Candace put her hand on Xavier's—"please stay. We're just having a light dinner—I'm going to grill a little salmon and some asparagus— and we'd love to have you eat here. Besides, Jack's looking for you, and he'll be so sorry if he misses you, and you know David doesn't get out so much these days and he'd love the company…"

Candace laid out her reasons that Xavier should stay to dine, and then, with a wink, withdrew her hand. Xavier laughed—"Do you know how hard it is to say no to you, Candace?"

"Well, then, don't!" she said, as if this were the perfect solution to their disagreement.

"Well, then, you'll have to call my wife and tell her why I'm late getting home when she's got all the kids there for the meal tonight."

"Oh, my," Candace said, caving, "I know how rare it is to get all the kids together after they're grown." She rose from her chair to see him to the door. "What's the occasion?"

David reached for Xavier's outstretched hand. "Something to do with becoming a grandmother for the first time, I assume?" he asked.

"You know, then," Xavier said.

"Everybody in Miami knows. And I also know" —he rolled his eyes toward Candace—"how grandmothers can be as overcome with the nesting instinct as the actual parents are. Candace had the nursery ready in this house before Abe's wife was three months gone with her first."

"I was being practical," Candace offered in her own defense. "There was a sale at Pottery Barn…"

"May I have a raincheck, Candace?"

"Certainly. Tell Mim we send our love."

Chapter 27

I had never before wanted so badly to hang up a phone, but of course that was impossible, what with my hands chained to my waist, so I did the next best thing: I grabbed the dirty, twisted yellow cord and pulled it as tight as I could and yanked it hard.

At least, I hoped that was the next best thing; I assumed ripping the phone out of the wall counted for disconnecting a call on a landline. Who knew how landlines worked these days? Chester Cruet was likely among the last owners of one of them in the contiguous United States.

When you know you have just made a ridiculous mistake, it is often accompanied by a physical reaction. If the mistake is small, without grave consequences, you cringe. A bit bigger, you might slap your forehead. Even bigger, maybe you swear, scream, kick something. But what I knew in my bones, without a shred of hard evidence to back up the presumption, was that I had just spoken with my kidnapper. That my kidnapper was in possession of Jack's phone. And, if the cheesy French guy had Jack's phone, did that mean Jack was in danger too? I had never before made a mistake quite this big and, while my brain processed the consequences of it from a far more rational place than I might have imagined possible, my stomach reacted of its own accord and I threw up a disgusting mess of pistachios and vodka and Coca-Cola and bile on the floor of the Cruets' kitchen.

I actually felt better after I'd emptied my stomach, only incredibly thirsty and desperate to get the taste of puke out of my mouth. I twisted my head to wipe my mouth on the shoulder of my jacket and made my way to the kitchen sink. I saw the faucet—one of those that had a single handle that needed only to be pushed back for the water to start flowing—and I took it as a gift from God. I bent over and butted my head against the handle and stuck my head under the tap and drank my fill. The water was warm—I could not manage to twist it to get it run cold—but it was delicious. I took a breath, and then drank some more.

I was unable to catch the handle again when I was done. It was too far out of my reach and, while it crossed my mind to try to find an implement to hold in my mouth and whack the handle back into its closed position, I also knew I had to get out of the Cruets' house. I had just given my kidnapper a glaring clue to my location, and I'd used any grace period I might have had rinsing my mouth and getting a drink. "Sorry," I said, an apology to Charlotte and her father for leaving the water flowing and running up their utility bill.

And for the nasty mess on the floor.

And the rest of the mess I'd made of their little kitchen.

The idea of going back out into the dark night, still shackled, made me shiver, though I understood that staying put was a worse notion. The immediate problem was, where would I go? Running between the shadows in Little Havana wasn't a solution; not with my captor in the neighborhood trying to spot me. Besides, it would be daylight at some point, and where would I hide then? No, no, no, I had to find a way to get to a telephone. Get in touch with— No, not the Cohens. I could tell them anything, certainly, but this news would better come after the fact. *Xavier.* I needed to find a phone and telephone Xavier.

The thought that Xavier would react rationally to my predicament and set in motion whatever rescue was necessary buoyed me, and I set out—

"*Jesus Christ*," I cried as I fell.

I wasn't sure how long I was out, possibly only seconds, but it was obvious what had taken me down: the fucking chain dangling from my wrists. I'd hit the table on my way to the floor, banged the edge of it with my right temple and hit the linoleum hard as I had no use of my arms to break my fall.

I scrambled to my feet, stunned at the amount of blood pooled on the floor where my head had rested but without the will or the time to investigate my latest wound. I wasn't dead and that was good enough for the moment. I reeled in the treacherous dangling chain and set out.

Chapter 28

THE convenience store looked shabby even through the most jaded lens, the front windows completely taken up with colorful ads for the products sold within—sodas, beers, chips, tobacco products—all of them featuring smiling, good-looking Hispanic faces, in recognition of the neighborhood in which the store was located. Most of the ads were also in some stage of decay, faded and peeling and graffitied, a mustache on that man selling a soda, a penis pointed at the mouth of that woman promoting a beer. There was a crumbling brick planter or fire pit or something that had been meant, at one time, to lend some aesthetic appeal to the sad, box of the structure, and thick metal poles—at one time painted red; now, like so many of the ads, faded and chipped and spray-painted with graffiti—placed strategically in front of the windows, designed to keep a car from gunning through the small lot, overshooting one of the eight parking spaces, crashing into the store itself. The lot was pocked with potholes and filled with debris—candy wrappers and hot dog boats and soda bottles and one sad, shriveled condom kicked into the gutter by a pad-locked ice machine outside the front doors.

Francisco took it all in with a shrug. He noticed a single employee—a lanky, slouching kid—moving around outside the back of the building, carrying an over-sized black bag of trash in either hand, swinging his arms high to toss first one and then the other into a dumpster; he thought about running inside and scooping up a snack while the kid was dealing with the garbage—his upbringing had made him loathe to give up a such opportunity: you ate when you found food in this world—but he remembered that he'd come a long way from those days, and he wasn't really that hungry, and why take the risk if he didn't have to? The convenience store was sad, but the small parking lot off to one side of it was ripe with possibilities. It was, moreover, unattended and ill-lit—the light from a streetlamp flickered into its first few rows, but other than that it was, happily, shrouded in the dark of night. Francisco had left his rental car parked on a side street—the doors unlocked and the keys still in the ignition, in the hope that it might be stolen and matters further confused when the law eventually got its hands on the vehicle. He jogged into the lot. It wasn't paved —perhaps it wasn't even a formal lot, more of an ad hoc area for neighbors to stash their rides if parking was at a premium on their street. His feet crunched over gravel and the overflow of garbage blown into the lot from what had been discarded in front of the convenience store next door. He moved among the rows of cars and trucks, most of them older models, choosing his new ride. He moved carefully past the later models—they were more likely to have car alarms, and those fucking alarms could be hair-trigger sensitive—and settled on a once-dark green 1990 Buick LeSabre with rust spots on the trunk lid but tires that passed a kick test and seemed reliable. No one was going to notice this bucket rolling down the street. Never had a man been more practical when making the choice of a new car.

Francisco took off his jacket, wrapped it around the brick he'd pilfered from the planter or firepit or whatever the thing was in front of the convenience store—a nod to muffling the sound—and drew back his arm to pound the brick against the back driver's side window. It shattered and he reached inside, popped the lock, slid into the seat and reached under the steering wheel.

Xavier noticed his cell phone flashing with a message even before he got in his car. He sighed and bent over to retrieve the phone—might as well enjoy the fresh air and balmy breeze for a few more minutes while he checked out the call, before he folded himself into the driver's seat for the long ride home.

"Christ," he said when he realized he'd missed fourteen phone calls—one from his wife, asking him to pick up a few items she'd forgotten at the grocery story on his way home—a loaf of sourdough bread and a bottle of sparkling apple cider so their pregnant daughter-in-law could toast with them when they popped champagne with the evening's appetizers, and thirteen from a couple of numbers he didn't recognize.

He played the first message. "Xavier," he heard Jack's voice say, "it's Jack. I need to know if you've seen Clint recently. He's—he's late coming home and I need to track him down." Xavier laughed; he had, indeed, seen Clint and he was lucky he wasn't late because he was passed out in a back alley, sleeping off his afternoon martinis. If not for his bodyguard giving him a lift, he probably would be.

And then he listened to the rest of the messages, some from Jack and some from Charlotte Cruet, none of them offering any details at all about why they were concerned about Clint being late, but each of them pleading for a return phone call made with increasing urgency. He'd paced through six of the messages before he too grew alarmed and dialed back. He let it ring until it went to voice mail and, rather than leave a message, he hung up and scrolled through his recent calls to find the other strange number from which he'd been receiving calls. Try that number. Before he could find it, Candace called to him from the front steps of the house.

"Xavier?"

"Oh, yes…"

"I saw you pacing out here—I thought I'd come out to see if everything is all right."

He couldn't think of what to say to her. What he could tell her that wouldn't alarm her too; he was an attorney and it went against every bit of his training, not to mention his scruples, to cause a client to feel alarm, especially when he himself didn't know if there was an absolute need to do that. "Just enjoying the night air." He held up his phone. "Checking messages..." Then he looked at her and noticed that she looked as agitated as he felt. "But, you, Candace... Is everything all right for you?"

Candace waved her manicured fingers, as if to dismiss herself. "We decided to turn on the news." She chuckled. "That's always a bad idea these days, isn't it?" She rolled her eyes. "There's been a shooting at a bar over in Little Havana. Apparently one of the patrons just pulled a gun on his companion and shot him, right in front of all the other patrons."

Xavier felt the muscles in his chest seize, though he tried to appear nonchalant—why in the world would a shooting in Little Havana, of all places, have anything to do with why Clint was late coming home? "Any other details?" he asked.

"No, no," Candace said. "The police aren't releasing any information, no names, all we know is what the local reporter is getting from the patrons. Apparently, the shooter just got up and walked out, if you can imagine the nerve."

Francisco tapped the steering wheel, bouncing to the beat and humming along to an old Ruben Ramos tune on the radio—he had a fondness for the classics, and appreciated the good taste of the anonymous owner of the vehicle he was driving. He leaned forward in his seat to read the street signs, and turned left onto Flagler Street, slowing to look for number 4344, the address that had come up for Chester Cruet when he'd pulled over and called directory assistance. "Hola, Chester," he chuckled when he noticed a light was on at the back of the house. "Who's home with you? Maybe Clint Kennedy?" He laughed as he pulled up to the curb just as the song ended and the disc jockey interrupted the broadcast with breaking news. It destroyed Francisco's mood, like a needle scratching over a record, until he listened to what the disc jockey was saying: there had been a shooting at The Latin Kitchen; the police were looking for a dark brown Mitsubishi four-door driven by a male, aged between eighteen and twenty-five, wearing a dark linen blazer, with short, dark hair and an immature beard. Immature? Francisco was incensed. He tipped the rearview mirror so he could look into it. His beard wasn't immature; it was well-groomed. Purposely short, bare on the cheeks and short but fuller at the jawline, a chin-strap style, very much in fashion. He tipped his head left, then right, scrutinizing his facial hair, and then he shrugged. Either way, the car the police were looking for had been ditched, the blazer was on the floor in the backseat wrapped around a brick, and he'd jump into Chester's bathroom for a quick shave as soon as he took care of other business in the Cruet house. He lifted his chin and picked with a fingernail at the dried blood on his neck. Maybe give his face a good scrub while he was at it.

Chapter 29

I saw the convenience store from across the street, from between the two parked cars, a dark blue minivan and an electric blue PT Cruiser, where I was crouched low. The place looked seedy as hell—one of the ratty posters that were plastered all over the front display windows featured a graffitied penis hovering above a model's open, smiling mouth. I saw a skinny young man—from what I could determine from peering around the posters on the windows, the store's only employee —leave the front counter and emerge a few minutes later from the back carrying two big black bags of trash, flinging one and then the other into a dumpster. When he'd rid himself of the garbage, he walked back over to the building, fished a pack of cigarettes and a lighter out of the back pocket of his baggy jeans, and lit up as he took a seat on what appeared to be an old pile of bricks at the side of the building. I enjoyed the infrequent cigar —mostly indulging only when I was with Pablo— but I hated cigarettes. Jack was the only person I knew who still smoked and I tolerated it in him in large part because he turned into a whining little bitch whenever anyone tried to tell him how bad it was for him. How it made him stink. In any other situation I would have taken one look at the sleazy convenience store and run the other way; right now, it looked like the safest haven I'd ever imagined.

I ducked back behind the minivan and, when the traffic allowed, zoomed across the street and into the dark between two houses about half a block up from the store. I made my way through the back yards, ducking behind trees and garages and, in one case, a dog house, in order to make a wide circle around that grubby little store and approach it from the rear. I took refuge behind a motorcycle parked in the driveway across the side street and peered at the back of the store. I could see at the side of it the silhouette of the employee still slouched on that pile of bricks, and I could see the back door standing just the way he'd left it: wide open and welcoming. Cue the "Hallelujah Chorus." I checked traffic and bolted across the side street and backed as hard and deep as I could into an overgrown hedge.

I stood there for several minutes, catching my breath, working up the courage to face the last hurdle—the spotlight that shone from the top of the store's back door. It was going to light me up like a fucking firework, if only for the few seconds it took me to dash through it, and it gave me— shall we say, *pause*—to even think about coming out of my hiding place and taking the risk. *Me*, risk adverse at last. Who'd have thought?

Then I saw the silhouette of the skinny employee toss his cigarette to the ground and unfold his body, stand up and stomp out the butt and turn toward the back of the store. My next move was total instinct: my body launched itself out of the hedge and I hauled ass toward that store, through the blinding light, into the back door and an exceptionally narrow hallway that reeked of urine mixed with bleach and led one of three ways: into the actual store, straight ahead, or into one of the two doors on either side. There wasn't a sign on either door, but scotch-taped on one was the notice that the restroom was for employees only, so I took a chance on that one, gripped the door handle, fumbling to turn it, open the door and get inside.

The room I was in had a strong smell of urine cake, so I was fairly certain I had actually entered the restroom. I turned around and faced the door, feeling the handle, praying to the gods that there was a lock on the door, and that it was one of those push-button types, not a hook somewhere higher up that I couldn't reach—and, thank you, Jesus, it was. I clicked the button softly as I heard the employee outside, in the narrow hallway, pulling the exit door closed behind him. I held my breath and offered up another prayer to the universe that the kid didn't have to take a piss, and I didn't exhale until I heard his footsteps pass the door and recede up the hallway and into the store.

I dragged my shoulders along the wall on one side of the door and, when I didn't find a light switch there, I dragged it along the wall on the other side of the door, where I ran into a shelf unit. My eyes were beginning to adjust to the infinite darkness—at least enough to sense that the shelves were filled with cleaning supplies and extra toilet paper and other such sundries—and I felt my way along it until, about four inches past the shelving, I realized I'd come to a corner, shifted myself to the right, and my fingers felt porcelain, a sink, which was progress, even as I involuntarily lifted my hands far away from whatever germs had congregated in its bowl.

Then I thought, Why the fuck are you so worried about a couple hundred thousand theoretical, microscopic organisms when you have a real, human-sized killer chasing your ass?

That's when I felt something tickle the top of my head. Something light and feathery and, nevertheless, so terrifying I almost screamed. And then I realized that it was a pull cord for an overhead light. And that, if I wanted light, I had no choice but to reach up, grab it between my teeth, and yank. I wondered how often the skinny kid upfront had entered this room, taken a whizz, and then pulled the cord to turn the light off without washing his hands. I used every bit of will power I could muster to banish the thought and did what I had to do.

I blinked hard when the light came on, closed my eyes until they could adjust to the brilliant glow, and prayed hard the kid upfront couldn't see it shining from beneath the door and wouldn't come back to investigate. When I could focus my eyes, the first thing I saw before me was a mirror, and my image in it, and I looked like hell. There was blood solidifying in my hair and streaked down the bruise turning purple on the side my face. There was more blood, as well as crusty brown puke, caked on my dove-gray jacket. My wrists were raw and bloodied too, and my hands were a sickly white, the only part of my body that, clearly, was not getting enough blood.

I let out a long sigh and maneuvered myself over the sink so I could turn on the cold water. The sink, let me point out, was equipped with one of those taps you found only rarely in America these days—two faucets, one for cold and one for hot —and I opted for the cold water because I didn't know how hot the hot water might run in this joint and, on top of everything else, I didn't want to scald myself.

I ducked my head into the bowl and let cold water run all over it. It was freezing, and refreshing, and I was shocked at the intensity of the red color that flowed from it, and how long it took for the water to run pink and, finally, clear. Then I turned my head and let the water rinse over my face. I checked the mirror to see if there were any glaringly obvious patches of blood still lingering, and the only one I found was inside my right ear but, without the use of my hands, there wasn't much I could do about that. I wished there had been one of those blow dryers in the room, the sort you often see in public restrooms but, alas, there was only a stack of paper towels sitting on the back of the toilet that was adjacent to the sink... I took a second look at the toilet. Yeah, I needed to use it. Funny how stress can make a person forget about things like having to pee.

I washed my hands a second time, and then shook them as best I could to dry, and I shook my wet head too, like the lead singer in some hair metal band, to get it to fall into some semblance of order. I did not, surprisingly, face any sort of dilemma about whether to flush the toilet or not; normally it would not have been a question, but I was not about to blow my cover with a rush of water, for the sake of flushing away a little piss.

What concerned me was my filthy jacket. I would have loved to take it off and ditch it in the overflowing trash can in the corner, but it is impossible to take off a sport jacket when your hands are cuffed to a chain around your waist. Not that I didn't take a moment to try to puzzle it out— as a kid I had once solved one of those "executive puzzle" contraptions—three metal rings that, when looped through each other in a tricky way, would form a circle rather than a line, or some such outcome. David kept a boatload of that sort of thing in his office so Jack and Abe and I would have ways to entertain ourselves when we visited his office. But, short of turning into Harry Houdini, who might have succeeded where I was clearly failing, or ripping the seams, which would have required an implement I didn't have at my disposal, I was stuck with the jacket. I could, however, untuck it—the exertions of the day had already pulled half of it on the other side of the chain that wound tightly around my waist, and I wiggled and stretched until the rest of it lay on top of the chain too. The jacket was still filthy, blood-ied and puked upon, but if I folded my hands just so over the length of chain reeled into them, and kept them primly in front of me, my loose jacket provided a bit of camouflage and it was no longer immediately apparent that I was trussed up like a common felon.

"OK, buckeroo," I said to the guy in the mirror. "Time to go up front and see if we can sweet talk that skinny kid into letting us use his phone."

Chapter 30

CHESTER Cruet rarely stayed out so late. He was
a gardener; he began his days early, and he
filled them unstintingly with the physical labor
his trade required. That morning he'd been at
the Cohens' house by 5:30 AM, in order to give
Candace's prize rose bushes the soaking they required well before the burning morning sun would
make the enterprise a losing one. He'd climbed
up and down a ladder all through the morning
heat, trimming the twelve-foot privacy hedge that
surrounded the Cohens' pool. He'd taken an hour
of shade in the potting shed at high noon, eating
the tuna salad sandwich and drinking the ther-
mos of strong, black coffee he'd prepared for his
lunch, transplanting aromatic herbs into terra
cotta containers for the Cohens' kitchen patio in
between bites and sips. In the afternoon he'd
blown the debris from the patio off the master
bedroom, scrubbed it down, hosed off its teak
chaise lounges and their plump yellow cushions,
planted fresh thyme in between the slabs of slate
so that when Candace Cohen stepped out to have
her morning coffee its scent would be released

under her tread.

There wasn't much Chester Cruet would not have done for the Cohens. He'd come to America as part of the Mariel boatlift in 1980 and, if not for the help David Cohen had offered him on his bumpy landing—giving him a job taking care of the grounds of his estate, helping him to obtain a mortgage for this cozy house in Little Havana, laundering the fifty thousand he'd managed to smuggle out of Cuba with him and turn it into legal United States tender—he would not have been able to make a life for himself and his family in this country. He owed the Cohens much, and he would spend the rest of his life trying to pay back their kindness, though this sort of repayment, he often mused to himself, had never been a condition of the Cohens' consideration. They were, without a doubt, the most decent people Chester could have hoped to live among in his new country.

He had been exhausted when he'd finished work this afternoon, but there was nothing that was surprising about that. He was often ready to just plop down on the sofa with a cold beer when he got home and watch television until he fell asleep waiting for Charlotte to call him for dinner. The hot sun was an energy sapper, and more so after every birthday. Not that he was an old man—he was certainly spry enough—but working outside eight to ten hours a day for so many decades had weathered him; he looked a good bit older than calendar years might have suggested. That night he was glad his daughter wasn't going to be home when he got off work. He loved Charlotte; however, her deception of the Cohens had shamed him. That she was now making amends and trying to get her life back on track gladdened him. That she was spending time these past few days with Clint and Jack neither particularly pleased nor displeased him, he was just happy they could carve out a friendship for themselves after the trouble Charlotte had caused. Had Charlotte been home this evening, however, she would have been busy in the kitchen, making a lovely dinner for them to share. And while he loved their evenings together, he was a little relieved that his evening nap could last as long as he wanted it to. He wouldn't be woken up to eat, make conversation, and then feel guilty when Charlotte refused to let him help clean the kitchen.

Still, when his neighbor had knocked on his door earlier and announced that he'd won a grand on a scratch-off lottery ticket he'd bought from that seedy convenience store a few streets over, and that he was buying the drinks, Chester felt he couldn't dampen his friend's happiness. A few beers to celebrate the man's good fortune—he mustered the energy to be a good neighbor.

As he returned home, driving down Flagler, he noticed the old LeSabre parked on the opposite side of the street. You didn't see cars of that vintage very often these days. Vintage cars of any make or model reminded him of Cuba, when he was a boy, and the LeSabre made him smile now. He also noticed that the light was on in the kitchen; Charlotte must already be home, he thought, though he hadn't seen her car on the street... And it was odd that she'd locked the front door behind her. "Charlotte," he called. It wasn't their habit to keep the door locked when they were home. It irritated him that he had to fish around in his pocket for his front door key.

He was stunned, at first, when he saw the wreckage in his kitchen. The water running in the sink, the phone pulled from the wall. The broken glass from the pane in the door all over the floor. The blood underneath the dining table. "Charlotte!" he shouted, fearful for her safety, because who else's blood would be on their kitchen floor? He put a hand to his heart. Moved toward the wall phone to call the police. Remembered that the phone was useless. Reached into a chest pocket of his work shirt and pulled out his cell phone. Turned around and around helplessly as he opened the flip phone. Gasped when the sound of water running stopped and he turned around once more and found a stranger standing by the sink.

Chester Cruet had not locked the front door behind him, and it had been easy enough for Francisco to enter his house. He'd moved so slowly and silently into the kitchen, hoping to surprise Chester just as he had. He giggled when Chester gasped and did that little hop upon discovering him. It reminded him of sneaking up on his mother when he was a little boy and scaring her so much it made her scream. It was one of the very few memories he had of her, and it always made him laugh.

"You should put down that phone, old man," Francisco advised. His Glock was trained on Chester.

Chester might have obeyed, but he found that fear had frozen him. He forced his mouth to move. "Where is my daughter?" he demanded.

Francisco shrugged. "Don't know." He lunged toward Chester and knocked the phone from his hand. It landed in the pool of blood on the floor, skidding a little, splashing a little of the gore onto the leg of Chester's work pants. "Don't care," Francisco added. "What I do care about is where is Clint Kennedy?"

Chester's eyes narrowed. His lips thinned.

"Old man! Tell me where is Clint Kennedy," Francisco repeated.

Chester swallowed.

Francisco took a step toward him and smacked the gun across his face. "One more time. Tell me where is Clint Kennedy."

Chester felt blood on his face. Felt it drip from the stinging place over his right eye. "Don't know," he replied. He pulled the handkerchief from his back pocket and wiped his wound. "Don't care."

"Huh," Francisco said.

And fired.

Francisco stepped over Chester's body as he made his way out of the kitchen. It was funny, he thought, how calm he felt. He had been nervous as a kitten, sitting in the bar across from Henri, talking about how to get money for Clint Kennedy from the Cohens. Sure, the kind of money Henri had been talking about was appealing to him, and he would have loved to have half a million all for himself, but the details of the ransom scheme had made him tense. Obscured his focus.

He walked through the Cruets' living room, toward the back of the house where a short hallway led to two small bedrooms, and a bathroom that was larger than he would have imagined for a house this size. He had to open the medicine chest and a few of the drawers in the sink cabinet to find what he needed—a razor, a fresh blade. Some shaving cream. He rifled through it a second time, to see what sort of prescriptions Chester Cruet might provide to him, but a half-empty bottle of Lipitor was all he discovered. He sighed and turned on the faucet and adjusted the water temperature to something just on the far side of what he could stand, and splashed his face before shaking the can of shaving cream and lathering the foam on his face.

Money, he thought, was just fine, but it was not his primary motivation. He was in it for the kill.

Chapter 31

I walked carefully through the convenience store. I knew the skinny kid would not be expecting anyone to be roaming around the store who he hadn't heard come in—who hadn't made the little bell that hung above the front door tinkle and alert him of a customer's presence. I looked alarming enough, what with the blood and the vomit smeared on my jacket, and I didn't want to scare the crap out of him.

I was also cautious about who else might walk into the store while I was in plain view. Francisco, of course, though really any other customer walking into the store would have put me on the razor's edge—I had no clue, for example, what the French guy who'd answered my call to Jack might look like. I wanted a shelf between me and any pair of human eyes. A shelf to dive behind if I heard a cheesy French accent.

The store, fortunately, was easy to navigate. When I stepped out of the short hallway that contained the restroom, I saw that it was laid out in your basic grid, set in a rectangle, poster-laden windows on three walls and coolers with sodas and beers, juices and dairy all along the back. The checkout, where the skinny guy worked the register while stuffed inside in a small window between and under displays of chewing gum and chocolate candies, cigarettes and chew, lottery tickets, batteries, beef jerky and Bic lighters, was against the far windowed wall. I waited for the young mother to put her cardboard container of baby formula in the stroller, next to her sleeping child, and start on her way home, and for the teenager to stuff his change in his pocket and take his pack of Kools outside to light up, before I eased my way to the front of the store.

I stood near the checkout, by an end cap full of chips and Cheetos that I could jump behind if anyone else came through the front door, and got the attention of the skinny guy by clearing my throat and asking, "Hey, is there a phone around here I could use?"

The end cap hid me so well that the skinny guy had to look around and follow my voice to figure out where I was. I slipped around the side of the display, stuck my head into the tiny passage way between the check-out counter and the windowed wall, and wiggled my fingers—which I realized was only drawing attention to the chain around my wrists, so I stopped doing that and smiled.

"Hey, man," the kid said, taking in my battered, bloodied jacket, the bruise spreading on my forehead, "you been in a fight or something?"

I nodded. "Yes. Yes, I have been in a fight. I'd like to use a phone to call a friend to pick me up. Do you have one?"

The kid frowned at the novelty of my request. "I think there's a pay phone out front," he said, and added, "I think it works."

I kept nodding. "Yeah, well—" Given that my skull was about to collapse under the pressure I was feeling, it was hard to be clear-headed about what I wanted to say to him. To pick just one of the many reasons I didn't want to dick around with the relic of a pay phone just at that moment. "See, the thing is, I lost all my money in that fight I was in."

The kid's frown deepened.

I elaborated. "I don't have any change to put into the phone to make my call."

"Oh!" the kid said, getting it. "I can give you some money." He put his hand into the front pocket of his jeans and started to fish around for change, but the bell over the door distracted him. I ducked behind the end cap.

"Where can I get gas around here?" I heard a man ask. He spoke neither Francisco's Mexican-inflected English nor in his partner's cheesy-French accent, and I exhaled.

"Just stay on this street," the kid was saying, "and go two stoplights. You'll hit a Chevron station."

"Thanks," the man told him. I waited until the bell that tinkled with his exit to inhale again.

"So, you want this change?" the kid asked, looking around for me.

I turned to face him, gave him a smile I hoped looked nowhere as pained as I felt. "How about," I asked, "you just let me use the store phone?"

The kid frowned again. "I'm not supposed to do that."

I resumed nodding. "Sure, I get that. But this is kind of an emergency."

The kid looked around, thinking. Then, checking the security camera over the door, he turned to me, motioned me behind the counter and held a cordless phone out to me.

"Thank you," I said, taking the phone from him and quickly punching in Xavier's phone number. I glanced up and saw the kid's eyes get really big as he got a good view of the chains around my wrists. "You think you could just"—I waved the phone toward my head.

"Oh, yeah," the kid said, "sure," and he propped the phone between my shoulder and my ear, and I listened to it ring.

Chapter 32

Enio pulled into the Cohens' driveway just as Xavier and Candace were pulling the front door closed behind them. Jack jumped out of the car before it had come to a complete stop, still holding the phone to his ear as he continued to shout at Xavier—"Oh, my God, thank God we got hold of you"—and stumbled up the stairs after them.

"Jack!" Candace gripped her son's hand with her own. "Hang up. You're here. We can hear you."

"Right."

"Jack"—Xavier paused a moment to wait for Enio to put the sedan into park, and for him and Charlotte to join them on the portico. His hesitating infuriated Jack, but this was simply Xavier being efficient, being a lawyer, making sure all of his witnesses were on the same page, and would therefore give corroborating testimony. "Look, Jack, what evidence do we have that Clint is actually in trouble? I mean, he's just late getting home, right? Which doesn't surprise me as the last time I saw him he was falling down drunk. I had to absolutely pour him into the car with that other bodyguard of his—"

"Francisco," Enio said.

"Yes, whatever his name is. Have you checked with him? Maybe he knows where Clint is."

"This is the problem," Enio said.

Xavier and Candace looked at Enio, waiting for him to go on.

"So please, tell us, Enio. My husband is recovering from a stroke and I'm not going to go in there and tell him Clint is missing and get him upset unless there's a good reason to—"

"Francisco is not his bodyguard, I think," Enio said.

Candace composed herself. "All right. Why do you think that?"

"I suspected for a while, but this afternoon, after the shooting—"

"The *shooting*?" This from Xavier.

Enio looked at Jack, and then at Charlotte, unsure of how much detail he should provide.

"What about the shooting?" Jack prodded him.

"The bullet I took from Charlotte's arm—"

Candace gasped and reached out for the hand of the younger woman, who was standing beside her.

"—and the one I took from the wall, at the house? The one fired by the assassin, and one of the ones Francisco fired back? They are the same kind of bullet. And the kind of bullet to use in Francisco's gun."

He paused, to let that sink in.

Tears sprang to Candace's eyes. "So. Someone is trying to kill him?"

Xavier looked as if he needed to sit down on one of the portico steps. "And I put him in the car with the man who wanted to do it...?"

Francisco felt his face, smooth as if he were just twelve years old, which was nice. But when he looked in the mirror over Chester's sink, he thought he preferred himself with a beard. He shrugged; it was just hair and it would grow back. He rinsed off the razor and put it in the trash basket, ran some water to rinse out the sink and wiped it dry with a hand towel he'd taken out of Chester's cabinet.

It was time to regroup. His target had gotten away. For now. He couldn't go back to Mexico until he had corrected this mistake—at least, he would not want to have to stand before Mateo until he had. He needed to relax and have a few drinks and a nice big bump before he could think about what his next move would need to be, and he knew just where he could do this.

He took the steps two at a time on his way down the stairs—not because he was in a particular hurry, but because he felt buoyant—a man with a plan! He let himself out Chester's front door and whistled while he jogged to the LaSabre at the curb.

Candace and David, Jack and Xavier, Charlotte and Enio sat at the island in the kitchen, each absorbed in his or her own thoughts, a gathering so quiet that Henrietta, David's nurse, backed out of the room and started upstairs again rather than disturb them to ask if there was anything else she could do before she went to bed. She met Elinda, the nanny to Abe's kids who were living with the Cohens while their father served his jail sentence, on the second-floor landing. "Don't go to the kitchen. Something's going on," she advised. "Better we stay out of the way."

"But Mrs. Cohen, she likes me to tell her when the little ones have gone finally asleep."

"I don't think she will care tonight. Come on," Henrietta said, and urged Elinda back up the stairs.

Francisco had made it to Homestead in about forty minutes, and he navigated now to one of the city's main thoroughfares, 296th Street, on his way to the Miami Homestead General Aviation Airport. The airport, which lay about three miles outside of the city limits, was a mixed-use facility—on any day one could find every sort of aviation activity, from jets coming in for a landing to skydivers falling from the sky; it was, indeed, where Clint Kennedy's pilot had landed his Gulfstream when they'd arrived in Florida just a day ago. It was also where the late Henri Bech, AKA Henry George Bechdel, the faux Frenchman who'd smuggled for Mateo for fifteen years—and never once been caught in the act—stowed the planes he used for business: five in all, including the 2006 Cessna 162 that was his go-to craft and the

1949 vintage Piper J-3 Cub that he'd considered the pride of his fleet.

Importantly, the Miami Homestead General Aviation Airport abutted the Everglades National Park, where Henri sometimes lived, albeit illegally, deep in the swamps with the 'gators and the crocs, in a hut he'd constructed. The hut was built on stilts, a more-or-less effective consideration against infiltration by various swampland creatures, and, for all its treehouse ambiance, was actually a rather sturdy construction, though the hut did lack all modern amenities. No running water; no electricity. No wifi. Henri had amassed all the money he'd need to enjoy quite comfortable living arrangements—in fact, he spent most of his time checked into Miami hotels like the Mandarin Oriental and the Biltmore, where he enjoyed sleeping on mattresses that weren't filled with mold, taking long, hot showers with water pelting down on him from rainfall shower heads, and eating out at some of Miami's finest restaurants. But the hut had one luxury Henri could never have found in civilization: abundant privacy. When he found himself under scrutiny, he liked being able to slip away to his jungle hideaway. Francisco had been to the hut once, when he'd been sent to Florida to back up Henri on a run, and he intended to find it again now. He would hide out there until he figured out how to pin down Clint Kennedy and take him out so he could return to Mexico, and Mateo, with that victory. Maybe even search the hut for Henri's stash. He chuckled to himself at the idea that

Henri would have hidden his fortune somewhere in the middle of the Everglades, but—he shrugged —he himself had seen stranger things. All that good coke had to be somewhere, not to mention all of Henri's cash, and Henri was surely not the type to have dealt with banks. It was such a nice fantasy, Francisco thought, to dream of walking away from this job with a nice payday bonus like that.

Enio stood, rigidly at attention, before the glass patio doors in the Cohens' kitchen, staring out into the grounds of the estate. There were answers he was seeking to the pressing questions— Where was Francisco? How could he get his bare hands on the little fucker and wring his traitorous neck? Yes, answers existed, but he had no access to them. When had he begun to suspect that Francisco was not wholly Pablo's man? What clues had the careless Francisco left in his wake? What had stopped Enio from acting? Pablo's confidence in the new man? Even so, he was not normally an indecisive man—was he slipping? Getting soft? Should he call Pablo and tell him what was going on in Miami? Would Pablo have any information that would help resolve the problems —or would he just wake up his ailing boss for no other reason than to piss him off with Francisco's treachery and his own incompetence? Every thought was a torture and ended up as a dead end in his brain. He punched in Francisco's number once more in his cell phone, and once more it went straight to voice mail.

Candace reached out a hand and placed it on top of Jack's clenched fists, a silent acknowledgment that they were thinking the same thing: they had been greedy, and the failing had been grotesque—they had put the life of one of their family in jeopardy. Candace tightened her grip as she noticed that there were tears standing in her son's eyes.

David sat back in his wheelchair, his face lifted to the heavens, his eyes closed against his cruel thoughts: Clint might die this evening. He might already be dead. He could die without ever knowing—

David felt strong hands on his shoulders. Xavier's hands. He reached his good arm and patted the hand on his right shoulder. That Clint was a young man David not only thought of as his son —that Clint *was* his son—was a secret everyone in this room, save the distant Enio, shared.

And still they did not speak of it, only accepted David's lament: "This has gone on too long." He shook his head; he had respected Clint's mother's wishes for far, far too long. "God help us, if we manage to come through this night with our family intact, no more secrets," he said softly enough that only Xavier could hear.

"Of course," Xavier whispered to him.

And then his phone rang.

Chapter 33

We had prearranged, Xavier and I, that when my saviors arrived, they would find me in the for-employees-only restroom of the convenience store. The skinny kid who was tending the store had no problem with me hanging out back there for half an hour or so—actually, he seemed more disinterested than anything else, which I thought was remarkable; had that been me tending the store, I would have had a million questions for the guy with the chains wrapped around his wrists. At the very least, I hope I would have asked if the guy was hungry or thirsty. The kid was absorbed in something on his phone screen as I walked away and didn't see me open the door of one of the cooler cases and grab a bottle of water. He didn't see me nab a box of Wheat Thin crackers off a shelf. I know because I looked behind me and he didn't even glance up from his phone.

I locked myself back in the restroom and drank my water with my now-patented technique of lifting the bottle with my mouth and glugging from it. Here's a tip if you ever find yourself in a position to have to drink from a bottle without using your hands: grip it in your teeth and, when you've had enough, seal the opening with your tongue before you stop gulping or you'll drip it all over yourself. I yanked a few paper towels from the back of the toilet with my teeth and spread a layer of them on a space on one of the shelves, then I opened the box of crackers, dumped them on the towels, and bent to pick them up and get them in my mouth with my teeth. I felt both inelegant and resourceful. OK...I was starving.

The knock on the restroom door, when it finally came, filled me with both fear and hope, and it wasn't until I heard Jack's lowered voice on the other side—"Clint?"—that I allowed myself to feel relief. The emotion flooded me as I threw myself across the little room and ripped open the door. I basically fell into Jack's arms.

"Move, move," Enio insisted, not letting me rest in the embrace, prodding both of us out the back door that he held open, into the car that sat running just outside, Charlotte behind the wheel. Jack bundled me into the back seat and climbed in after me even as Enio ran back inside.

"Where's he going?" Charlotte cried.

"Security tapes," Jack answered, trying not to let me see he was horrified by my appearance, by the fact that my hands were chained. He got me situated by doing something as normal as buckling me into my seatbelt, but his hands were shaking so badly he couldn't get the buckle to snap.

"Jesus," Charlotte muttered, hunched over the wheel, impatient to hit the gas.

"Well, we can't leave videotapes of Clint all over Miami," Jack snapped back at her.

"Jack, how much money do you have?" I interrupted their spat to ask.

He sat back in his seat. "I don't know." He fished his wallet out of his pants and counted. "Two hundred bucks"—he fanned through a few smaller bills—"and change."

"Go give it to the skinny kid behind the counter."

He was so nervous he didn't even ask me why.

"I don't even want to know why you have these," I said.

We'd driven directly to Jack's place, where he retrieved a huge, orange-handled bolt cutter from the small utility closet on his terrace.

"Left over from a home renovation project, asshole," he answered me. "You use them to cut the mesh rebar reinforcement when you tear down a wall. Remember when that half wall used to be between my kitchen and the dining area?"

"Just cut me out of these." I sighed and jangled my chains, and Jack handed the tool to Enio, who did the job quickly. I would have reveled in my freedom, but Charlotte stepped in with gauze and adhesive tape and a big brown bottle of hydrogen peroxide.

"Jesus, what a mess. These cuts are deep."

I couldn't look at my wrists as she cleaned them up. I *felt* how deep and ragged they were with each burning application of the hydrogen peroxide, so I didn't need to see the wounds as well.

"Feeling squeamish?" she asked as I turned my head.

"More than I want to admit."

Charlotte nodded as Jack and Enio paced Jack's living room, Jack right to left and Enio left to right, both of them deep in their own thoughts and, for the moment, ignoring us. "You know," she said, "it could work."

"It could?" I asked. "What could?"

Charlotte shrugged, uncapped a tube of Neosporin. "You, having red wine every once in a while," she whispered.

It took me a moment to catch up with her. Once, when we had spoken of being together, Charlotte had cast herself as chardonnay, and the men she knew I was also attracted to as syrah. Would I—*could* I—limit my consumption to one or the other in consideration of a long-term relationship with one particular varietal? The question had confused me. Didn't every monogamous relationship entail the sacrifice of not merely every other varietal, but every other fucking *grape* on every other cluster of them the world over? I hadn't given the sacrifice a second thought when Taavi had been the subject of it; even I had seen Charlotte notice my hesitation when she asked me if I might be willing to make the sacrifice for her.

"I mean," Charlotte continued now. "I'm Cuban, remember? I'm used to our men having mistresses. And boyfriends. It happens, and we're adults, right?"

I smiled at her. And kept smiling as she tended to my wrists. Willing to concede only that we were both adults.

"Tell me everything," Enio said, striding to where Charlotte and I sat on the sofa, gathering up the chain from the floor where it had fallen and flinging it aside. "Everything that you did from the moment I dropped you off at Xavier's building to this moment now. Tell me something so we can find the bastard Francisco."

"Right," I said. And so I did, even the parts that weren't flattering to me. I admitted that most of the time between when I'd had my third martini and when I'd woken up on the floor of the garage in Little Havana was a blur. I didn't even really remember bumping into Xavier on the elevator. I explained how I'd managed my escape from the garage, found myself in Little Havana, got my bearings and made a run for it to Charlotte's father's house. How I'd been surprised to find that Chester wasn't at home, so I'd broken into the house and managed to place a phone call. In any case, nothing I said seemed to truly spark Enio's interest until I got to that part, standing in the Cruets' kitchen and trying to call Jack from their wall phone.

"So, it was Francisco who answered when you called that number?"

"No," I told him. I held my right arm at an angle so Charlotte could more easily dab Neosporin onto my wrist and wrap it, as she had the left, in layers of gauze. I looked like a mental patient who'd tried to slit his wrists when she was done, but her attentions had greatly soothed the pain. "Thank you," I said to her, feeling kindly toward her again, wishing the spell she'd had me under before she'd proved herself to be so adept at disposing of a dead body hadn't been broken but... I inhaled deeply, hoping to catch a whiff of her piney smell and caught—nothing. The spell was shattered, and just when she was warming to my affections, and that rather broke my heart for both of us.

"So? Who answered when you called Jack's number?" Enio insisted.

"I don't know." I shook my head to bring me back to the moment we were all sharing. "Somebody who thought he'd try to disguise his voice by putting on a French accent."

Enio had seated himself before me, on Jack's coffee table, and he leaned toward me now. "A phony Frenchman?"

I nodded. "Yeah."

Enio leaned back again. "I know this man."

"You know a phony Frenchman?"

"I do."

"Well, isn't that just helpful as fuck?" Jack snapped. "How does that help us to know where *Francisco* is?"

Enio ignored him. "And what happened when you talked to this Frenchman? What did he say to you?"

"Well"—I tried to remember his exact words, but the stinging sensation that had accompanied the realization that I was talking to my kidnapper had been too overwhelming and I couldn't recall.

Enio tried a different tack. "Well, then, what did you say to *him*?"

This I could remember vividly. "I didn't say anything to him. I yanked the phone cord out of the wall, you know, to disconnect the call." I shook my head. "I don't know what good I thought that was going to do—I mean, I was calling Jack's cell phone and the Frenchman had probably already seen Charlotte's name come up on the caller ID. I just knew I had to get out of that house as soon as I could because *now* they could easily track me down—find out where I was and come looking for me—"

Charlotte gasped and dove into her purse for her phone. She fumbled to flip it open and scroll through her contacts, but her hands had begun to shake so she just screamed at it, "Call Daddy!"

None of the rest of us even dared to breathe as the phone rang once—twice—three times.

Eight full rings and, as it went to voice mail, Charlotte looked at us, from one to the other, helplessly.

Enio took the phone from her and hung it up. "Maybe your father hasn't come home yet? Does he have a cell phone?"

Charlotte was already on the verge of sobs. "Of course, he has a cell, what number do you think I just dialed? And of course, he's home by now, the man wakes up to go to work at three-thirty in the morning, I'm worried why he was out of the house when Clint got there in the first place—"

Charlotte shuddered, and caught her breath and the rest of us held ours again, waiting for her to tell us what we were going to do next.

"I have to go home," she said, gathering up her purse and stepping over my legs and Enio's to get to Jack's door. She grabbed the door handle and turned around to us as she opened it. "For the love of God, will someone take me home!"

"Yes. Yes," I said—or *we* said. In any case, we stood in unison and followed her out of Jack's and back into David's car.

Chapter 34

THE Everglades covers over a million and a half total acres, and all but about two hundred thousand of those acres are designated as wilderness by the National Park Service—the largest tropical wilderness in the United States. This wilderness is made up primarily of sawgrass marshes and wet prairies—which are much like the marshes but with a greater diversity of plants. These are what people think of when they think Everglades. But, in truth, there are other sorts of vegetation within the park. There are, for example, tropical hardwood hammocks, small islands of trees that are slightly elevated between limestone plateaus or peat bogs beneath, natural fortresses that are good habitats for reptiles and some small mammals, but hard for humans to penetrate due to the razor-sharp saw palmettos that typically grow around their bases. There are cypress swamps, the largest of which—"The Big Cypress"—measures twelve-hundred square miles; pine rocklands, some of the driest terrain in the Everglades, the floor of which is covered with highly flammable dried pine needles—part of how the pines sustain themselves as fire that takes out competing vegetation is necessary to their survival; mangrove forests that grow in brackish water, where fresh and saltwater meet, absorbing the energy of the coastal waters, waves and storm surges, and serving as rookeries for birdlife and nurseries for fish and shellfish. It was the marshes—acres and acres of them—that fanned out from the town of Homestead and, in Francisco's memory, Henri's hideaway was dwarfed—hidden, really—among the damp and dark of a forest of trees. Cypress trees or mangroves; Francisco didn't know the difference, just that they were enormous.

On average, around a million people visit the Everglades annually, a total the National Park Service keeps track of by tallying the number of tourists who enter the park through its two entrance stations, one located in Shark Valley, and one in Homestead—this latter entrance fast approaching as Francisco drove the LeSabre toward the Miami Homestead Airport—though the park service openly qualifies this statistic by citing that there is really no way to keep track of those who may enter the park through the nearly half a million acres of water that surrounds it. Francisco tried to remember how he'd entered the Everglades with Henri the one time he'd been—he didn't think they'd entered by way of water, but they certainly hadn't ducked through any official-looking portal or visitor center where there were maps or brochures available. But what did he know? He and Henri had been snorting a boatload of coke on the plane ride into the US, so everything about the trip was both intense and fuzzy in his memory.

When Francisco had first started working for Pablo, Enio had caught him sampling the wares. Francisco had feared that he was going to say something about it to Pablo, but Enio's only response had been to say, "Drug smugglers who do coke have a fool for a dealer." Francisco had thought it was a clever remark, and he'd laughed when Enio said it. But he'd had the example Henri had set for him—fifteen successful years in the business. and coked up or worse for every day of it. He figured Enio needed to pull the stick out of his ass.

Per government tracking, most of the visitors who tour the Everglades are women—56% to 44%. And the vast majority—we're talking 64% —are over fifty years old. Francisco had looked this up on his phone and it made sense to him: Florida was a state with a lot of old people; it was filled with widows. What he couldn't figure out was why anyone other than a drug dealer on the run would want to visit the Everglades. He thought of himself as a city animal, and a place as uncivilized as the Everglades just scared the shit out of him—the terrain was unfamiliar, certainly, but it was the wildlife that really terrified him. It was filled with birds, of course—storks, ibises, spoonbills—and these he could take or leave so long as they left him alone too. But the alligators and the crocodiles, the panthers and the wild hogs—he reached his hand up to touch his shoulder holster and patted his gun. He hated the idea of those creatures, but he had the weapon to take them out if they bothered him. What really freaked him out were the snakes, not only the rattlesnakes and other sorts of slithering creatures that were native to the Everglades, but the Burmese pythons that were not. From what he'd read on the Internet, the pythons had been imported from Southeast Asia as pets and, when they were no longer wanted, were released into the swamps and marshes. They were fast breeders, thrived in the hot, tropical climate, and were up against no natural predators; so now they, or their offspring, had begun overtaking Southern Florida —estimates were putting the entire population at around ten thousand. Ten thousand pythons— the very idea made Francisco shudder. So many slimy, slithering snakes feasting on small, native mammals in the Everglades—rodents and rabbits and raccoons—that some of those small species were in danger of extinction. All those snakes, crawling along in the swamp waters just waiting to wriggle around the leg of an unsuspecting—

Was it really a hut? Henri's hideaway? Francisco tried to recall. Or was it more of a platform, built up on stilts, maybe with an overhang? Were Burmese pythons ground snakes, or did they climb into trees, wrap themselves around the low-hanging cypress branches? Was that where they waited for their unsuspecting human prey? He flashed to a scene from one of the few movies he'd seen as a kid, "The Jungle Book," and the snake character. Hadn't that been a python?

That motherfucker climbed everywhere. Swung from the goddamned treetops.

Maybe it was time to rethink his plans.

Francisco pulled off the road, into the lot of an IHOP, and parked the car. His fucking cell phone was ringing—Enio again. He tossed it on the passenger seat of his car and reached into the front pocket of his jeans to pull out his last amber vial. Half full—half full. He needed to get his hands on more. He should have taken the time to go through Henri's pockets before he left that bar. The other patrons were scared enough of him that he would have had thirty seconds to do that, or maybe he could have found out what hotel Henri was staying in because his stash was probably in his room, and, judging from the quantities Henri had been willing to share with him in the last few hours, it was probably a good-sized stash. Fucking idiot he was not to have done that, fucking idiot not to kill that fucker Clint Kennedy when he had the chance, should never have listened to Henri, fucking greedy bastard, they were drug dealers not kidnappers, should not have killed two people because now the police were looking for him, or they would be looking for him soon, and he was going to have to ditch the LeSabre too because sooner or later someone was going to report it stolen, then the police would find the LeSabre right by the Everglades and figure he was somewhere in the Everglades too, especially if the police connected him to Henri and they already were on to his hideaway in there, but where else could he go, not back to Mexico, not while Clint Kennedy was still alive, Mateo would shoot him himself and all for what, for the fear that the miserable tyrant Pablo was going to divide up the territories unfairly, redraw borders in favor of the little bitch Kennedy, give that gringo a chunk of business that rightfully belonged to a Mexican man who had been Pablo's business partner for decades, and what was that for, what was so special about Clint Kennedy and, anyway, Henri was his transport back to Mexico, so he was going to have to call Mateo at some point if he wanted to go home …

He had killed Henri. Henri! A major link in Mateo's transportation chain. This was going to be a problem for Mateo.

Mateo was going to make it Francisco's problem.

He had fucked up, he had fucked up everything, he had fucked himself—

The thoughts tumbling in his head sounded like voices coming from just outside the car, a woman calling to him from the black truck parked three spaces over, a man shouting to him from the front door of the IHOP, another man whispering to him from outside the driver's side window, but no matter how quickly he looked around he could not catch sight of any of them.

Francisco fumbled to unscrew the top of the vial, shook about half of the powder left within it onto the back of his hand, brought the shaking appendage to his nose and inhaled greedily, quickly, and then he sat, still and quiet, and enjoyed the silence, the power boost.

He couldn't remember the last time he'd slept. He needed to get his hands on something to perk him up or he was going to crash before his work here in Florida was done. He was going to have to stay here in the Everglades where it was going to be another shitty eight-five-degree day and steamy in the swamps. He needed to get his hands on something to help him endure it.

He felt his phone vibrate in his pocket.

Enio again.

This time he considered, briefly, answering.

Chapter 35

THE front door was standing open when we pulled up in front of the Cruet house. My breath caught when I saw that; I knew I hadn't touched the front door the last time I'd been to this house. Charlotte was trying to open the car door to get out even before Enio had brought the vehicle to a complete stop. I was in the back seat with her and I reached across and grabbed her around the waist before she could get her feet to the curb.

"Charlotte, wait—"

"What the fuck, Clint, let me go—"

"Please!"

I tried to pull her back into the car and, much to my surprise, she let me. "Enio," I said, even as he was already getting out from behind the driver's seat, "why don't you go have a look around first? Make sure everything's OK."

Jack had ridden shotgun. "I'll just stay here with you two," he decided.

"Of course," I told him. I didn't want to go into the house either.

We watched Enio walk up to the front door of the Cruet house and slip inside, and then we sat in the car in silence for what felt like an elongated time-out-of-time, but was, in reality, a matter of two or three minutes until Enio reappeared. I felt Charlotte sink back against me as Enio walked toward us, alone. Sink into me as if her very life force had slipped away.

Enio walked up to Charlotte's window, and Jack scrambled to push the button and roll it down so we could hear what he had to say. I wrapped my arms tightly around Charlotte before he could speak. "Francisco, I think, was here," he said.

I nodded. "Chester?"

Enio replied by shaking his head. I felt Charlotte's body spasm as she turned her head and buried it in my chest, but she uttered not a word, as if the effort of sound was beyond her.

We sat like that for another elongated moment, and then Jack asked, softly, "What do we do now?"

It was a rhetorical question. Enio turned his back to the car door. It looked to me as if he'd pulled his phone out of his pocket and was making a call, but I couldn't really see, and I didn't really care. It hit me how much there was to be done —how many decisions there were to be made at this juncture—but all I could think clearly about was Charlotte, and the grief I was holding in my arms. I didn't let go of her and I was glad I'd kept a grip because suddenly she pushed away from me and would have bolted from the car if Enio hadn't been standing right there, blocking her exit with his body.

That was when Charlotte found her voice again. A sound that seemed not to come from her but from the core of the earth itself, not loud but rumbling, and encompassing.

I waited for recrimination. I don't know what it says about me that a friend's father was dead and what I was worried about was that she was going to blame me for it. Or—to my credit—maybe what it says is that I was willing to accept that I *was* to blame. Own up to my responsibilities. I was the one who'd decided to save myself by breaking into her father's house. I was the one who called my kidnappers from the Cruets' phone and gave away the location.

I was the one who got everyone I cared about involved in this whole money-laundering scheme in the first place and put us all in danger.

These were the thoughts that were running around in my brain like a pack of howling hell beasts while Charlotte sobbed in my arms.

Enio bent down and leaned into the open car window. "We need to move," he said.

Right. But where? He could see the questions in my eyes and, with some hesitation—respect for the weeping woman in my arms—he said, "I could clean up in the house."

I felt Charlotte's whole body tense. She knew as well as I did what Enio meant, even if she didn't know the extent of the mess inside. Enio wanted to scrub my blood and vomit—as well as the less visible signs I'd been in the house, like fingerprints—from the kitchen; he wanted to put Chester's body in the trunk and dispose of it as he had done with the other body earlier in the day. It was so wrong on every level.

"Enio, that's her dad in there," I said. And I was going to allow absolutely nothing to get in the way of Charlotte's being able to mourn him, and bury him, and know where his grave was so she could visit it. "We have to call the police."

Enio drew in his breath and then he nodded. "In that case," he said to me, "the police are going to eventually trace this back to you. So we'll need to get you out of the country."

"For how long?" Jack squeaked in a voice that sounded as high as it had twenty years ago, before either of us had hit puberty.

I gave him a look, the sort that I hoped would both soothe him and silence him. Once the police got hold of this, my bet was that they'd be able to tie me to two murders—but I understood... hoped that if I wasn't around for questioning, if their trail went cold, maybe they wouldn't make the connection to the Cohens.

"Before we go, Enio," I said, "I'd like to track down the guy who's responsible for all of this grief."

"As would I," Enio agreed.

Jack leaned toward us, over his seat. "I'm going with you."

I closed my eyes, mainly so I wouldn't see Enio's reaction to Jack's declaration, and Charlotte whimpered. "Jack," I said, as calmly as I could, "think about this. Right now, there's nothing about this situation that can come back and bite you. We need to keep it that way."

I felt Charlotte turn her head, so it wasn't buried any longer in my chest but merely resting on my shoulder. She sniffed, and lifted a hand to wipe at her eyes. "That means," she said, sitting up, "you all need to get out of here."

"But—" I tried to think fast. If the three of us took off, that meant Charlotte would be left going into the house all by herself—

"Shut up, Clint. I want to go have a few minutes alone with my father." She wiped her cheeks with her fingers. "Then I'll call the police and come out and sit on the stoop until they get here." She patted my knee to stop me from objecting. "I'll be all right. You need to go so you'll be all right too."

Her kindness stabbed me. Wasn't I the one who'd, oh, so recently, felt let down by what a tough girl she had turned out to be? Now look who was benefitting from her strength. She leaned over and kissed my cheek. "I was wrong," she whispered to me. "It wouldn't have worked." She added, "Bye, Jack," before getting out of the car.

Enio stepped aside to allow her to open the door, and he walked her into the house while Jack and I sat there like the cowards we were. Enio stayed in the house with Charlotte for a good ten minutes. When he emerged, he jogged to the car, slid into the driver's seat, and we sped away.

Chapter 36

Henry George Bechdel, aka Henri Bech, had been born in a small Pennsylvania town in 1947, the son of an assembly-line worker at a factory that manufactured small, private planes. It was a company town in that, if one didn't work at the plane factory then one worked in support of those who did—kept a shop in the one-block downtown district, worked for one of the town's three doctors or two dentists, taught in one of the neighborhood schools. In 1964 Henry had dropped out of high school and taken up a place in the assembly line next to his father, but he had soon grown bored. His problem was that he was a smart kid, someone who might have been destined for farther horizons if his options hadn't been so geographically and culturally limited. His family had lived in the small town for seven generations; none of them had graduated from college, largely because none of them had ever even thought about attending one. Henry's saving grace had been catching the attention of his shift foreman, an old timer with a good heart and a long-standing relationship with both the company's pilots and the instructors who ran the flight school that shared the tiny airport. The foreman had made Henry a deal: if Henry would earn his G.E.D., the foreman would make sure he learned to fly. So motivated, Henry had quickly fulfilled his part of the bargain; within two years he'd earned his pilot's license and was hired by the company to deliver its product far and wide. His first solo delivery had been to Grand Rapids, Michigan, and his first delivery out of contiguous U.S. had been to Guatemala. Henry proved himself to be a reliable and conscientious employee and, from there, the world opened up to him. A delivery to the south of France—a relatively short trip that had provided just one overnight in the country—had turned him into a devoted Francophile, and left him with the remarkable, permanent affectation of that objectionable accent. A delivery to northern California had turned him on—sure, he'd smoked a little weed in his life, or maybe a *lot* of weed—but dropping acid was like coming home to a place he'd never known existed. A delivery to Montreal—a trip that was supposed to be an overnight with a quick turn-around— turned into a four-day binge when the man who, by that point, styled himself as Henri found out that the concierge at his hotel could hook him up and, subsequently, *that* turned him into one of the growing numbers who were left unemployed in the recession of 1975. Henri, however, had a bit of savings and celebrated his new-found freedom with a vacation in Acapulco. It was there he discovered a new outlet for his only marketable skill: he began smuggling drugs in 1976 and never looked back. In 1994, based on his stellar record of zero busts in almost twenty years, he began working for Mateo Martín, lord of Nuevo León—and, apparently, wanna-be lord of Tamaulipas. Henri's record had remained clean right up until he'd been found dead in The Latin Kitchen, a low-rent bar and grill in Little Havana earlier that night.

Enio filled us in on most of Henri's background—Henri was a bit of a legend in the drug business—and the news anchor on the television that was set above the breakfast nook in the Cohens' kitchen filled us in on the rest. An alarmingly accurate sketch of Francisco appeared on the screen, the visual to the anchor's warning that the shooter was still at large, and considered armed and dangerous.

"What are you going to do now?" David asked.

The Cohens had been stoic as I'd filled them all in on the events of the evening—or, at least as much of them as we could piece together at that point. Now all of us felt blindsided at the possible repercussions of what had transpired.

"I'm going to get on my plane and head back to Mexico," I said.

David nodded and then, as ever looking both ahead and out for me, said that I ought to check with Xavier, but he was fairly certain Mexico would allow extradition, if it ever came to that.

"I will, David," I told him, even as I wondered how eager Xavier would be to take my phone calls going forward. Not that I thought Xavier would ever completely shut me out, but he'd left shortly after I'd arrived at the Cohens and started telling my story—"I'm an officer of the court, Clint. You can talk to the Cohens, but you can't tell me these things," he'd said, and I'd felt a whole layer fall out from under the foundation of my life.

"But I think David's right, Candace—I mean, I expect they would extradite, and that going to Mexico is only a temporary solution for me." I saw the alarm in Candace's eyes, the tears welling, so I added, "It will be at least a few days until I'm linked to any of this. And maybe I never will be. We can't know at this point."

Candace waved a dismissive hand at me even as she stretched out her arms, grabbed me around the neck and hugged me as tightly as she ever had. "I'm crying because I'm upset about Chester. Thirty years he's been our friend—"

"I'm so sorry, Candace—"

"And I can't stand the idea that I don't know when I'll see you again—"

"Clint." David interrupted his wife. "I'd like to speak with you." He lifted his good hand and pointed toward the kitchen door. "Wheel me into my office, will you?"

It had been over a decade since I'd been directed into what David called his office, which is a fairly large and sunny room with grass paper and important art on the walls, and an imposing teak desk set in front of a large bay window. I'd been in this room plenty of times as a kid, frequently with Jack, often when Candace had caught us in

some bad act and, in addition to whatever punishment she herself meted out to us, insisted upon
our confession to her husband. Those confessions
had been excruciating, because David was, without fail, more disappointed with us than he was
angry. The last time I'd been there had been the
night before I'd surrendered myself to serve the
jail sentence I'd earned in my early twenties, when
I'd been busted for running a high-end escort service. That night my audience with my father-figure had been typically excruciating, though exaggerated because he'd wanted me to know that he
was proud of me for accepting with such grace the
punishment the state had meted out to me. I can
handle most anything except a pep talk.

"Close the door," David said to me after I'd
wheeled him where he wanted to go, which was
behind the big desk. He gestured for me to take a
seat on the other side of it. "First things first." He
slid a couple of sheets of paper and a pen across
the desk. "The agreement for Candace to take over
custodianship of Elmer. Let's make that official."

"Yes," I said, picking up the pen and not bothering to read before I signed.

I slid the papers back toward David. "Good," he
said. "Now, there's something else we need to talk
about."

"Sure. Of course," I said, and prepared myself
for pain.

Chapter 37

THERE is a school of thought that says knowing the identity of one's biological parents is a basic human right. At least that's one interpretation of what Article 8 of the European Convention on Human Rights provides, although it comes with its own caveats—the knowledge should be acquired lawfully, and be respectful of the necessities of a democratic society as a whole.

I had known my mother well, admired her intensely and loved her dearly. She'd raised four boys—my three older brothers and me—single-handedly, earning her living by working every weekday as the housekeeper for Candace and David Cohen and keeping her own house spic-and-span by instilling a sense of responsibility in all her sons. God help us if our beds weren't made or our socks weren't in a hamper or our dishes were left in the sink, mostly because it would never have occurred to any of us that these chores would be accomplished if we didn't do them for ourselves.

My need to know my father had been well met by a solitary, faded Polaroid photograph in a brass frame my mother kept on a shelf in the living room, and the stories my three older brothers told about the fellow in the photo—a slender and rather handsome man in a polo shirt, madras shorts, and leather sandals standing next to a shiny, bronze-colored 1979 Chevrolet Camaro Z28.

"He never let anyone else drive that car."

"He loved that car."

"At least he could love *something*."

It was my brothers who told me how he'd left our family home several months before I was born but, as no one else seemed to be terribly curious about where he'd gone when he'd left, I wasn't either. Where Dad was had never been presented as a family mystery; in general, my mother and my brothers seemed happy enough just to have him gone, so I was too.

My brothers and I were never very close. Charlie and Rich and Leo were nine, ten, and twelve years older than I was, respectively, so it wasn't any sort of failing that we'd never bonded, as brothers nearer in age might have. By the time I was starting first grade, Leo was in El Salvador, part of a U.S. deployment to assist in training government forces in counter-insurgency. The year I started third grade, Rich was starting his first year at Florida SouthWestern State College and his work on an associate's degree in physical therapy. Charlie—the one of us who everyone said looked the most like our handsome father—left home for Los Angeles the summer before I entered fourth grade, with dreams of becoming an actor or a model.

We all still keep in touch, calling on each other's birthdays and sending Christmas cards—Charlie's from L.A., where he is a successful voice-over actor; Rich's from Colorado Springs, where he specializes in sports injury rehab, and Leo's from wherever he has lately deployed. The last time we'd all been together in one place at the same time, however, was at our mother's funeral, nearly thirteen years before. I was just twenty-two then, and a recent college graduate. My brothers had teased me—gently but relentlessly—about my fancy degree. They'd taken charge of organizing our mother's service, though David Cohen was the one footing the bill, and I was glad to let them all do whatever it was they wanted. I was buckling with grief and happy to defer to their greater age and experience and, in turn, they made sure to include me in all the discussions we had to have about the details—what kind of flowers to have on her coffin, which charity were memorial donations to be directed. The day after the funeral, when we were cleaning out Mom's house, they gave me first pick among the items each of us wanted to take to remember her by. I chose the small ruby birthstone ring she wore on her right ring finger on the rare days when she wasn't going to have to plunge her hands into a bucket of soapy water. At the end of the day of clearing out, the only thing that remained unclaimed, neither in a pile for one of us boys or the larger pile for Goodwill, was the solitary, faded photo of our father in the brass frame. "Let Clint take it," Leo had laughed, setting the others off. "Yeah, give it to Clint," Rich had chuckled. "Clint never knew him," Charlie agreed between giggles, "which is why he's the only one who'd want it."

I still had the ruby, now part of a pair of cufflinks I'd had made and wore when I dressed in black tie, and I still had the photo, too, I was fairly sure, likely in one or another of the boxes gathering dust in the storage room of my house in Mérida.

I had adored my mother, and continued to share affection if not great love among my brothers, but the Cohens were my family.

"There really would have been no good time to have this conversation," David said from behind that massive desk in his stately home office. "At least, I haven't found a good time in the last thirty-five years and, now that it's come right down to it, it's particularly awkward..."

I let him go on, but I already knew what he wanted to say. Had probably always known. I let him go on because I appreciated David's need to say it out loud—it was another indication of the seriousness of my fate—but I was so grateful when his words slowed and came to an end in that open-ended ellipse.

I did, however, want to know *why*.

"Why wasn't I ever allowed to know? Was it Candace? You didn't want to hurt her?"

David shook his head. "Candace has known from the first, for as long as she has loved you, Clint, and that's been all your life. That woman taught me everything I know about forgiveness."

"But— Did you love my mother? Did you ever even love her?"

"Do you mean, did we have a grand affair?" David smiled. "I'm not sure that was a consideration for either of us. Your mother's husband had just left her, though most of us were surprised he'd stayed as long as he did. He was a ladies' man with wanderlust—a fatal combination. Candace and I were going through a rough patch, trying to work things out between us." He smiled again. "Your mother and I were friends, Clint. And we made a mistake." He shook his head and said, "And Candace saw no reason to destroy the lives of those three young boys she adored, just because two adults had acted impulsively. She and your mother were friends too, Clint. And she thought you deserved to grow up with your father in your life."

I shook my head now with disbelief. "But why couldn't *I* have known that? That I was growing up *with* my father?"

David sighed. "Because that was what your mother wanted. She didn't want your brothers to think even less of their father. Or of you. Or of her, come to that. To have to carry that baggage."

I nodded, understanding, as much as that was possible, and looked across the desk, at David— the man I had always viewed as a father-figure. I was a man about to lose my country, and I was leaving behind a life that had never actually been mine.

Chapter 38

Dᴀᴡɴ hadn't yet broken by the time Enio and I made it to our destination. We'd talked about swapping out cars at the Cohens', at Candace's insistence: "If that worm, Francisco, is looking for you, he'll be looking for David's car. Take my putter-around"—the silver-blue Mercedes SL 450 Roadster she used for puttering around town to run errands—"and Jack can drive me to pick it up tomorrow."

Enio had spent most of the last twenty minutes that we'd been at the Cohens' house standing outside in the chill of the coming dawn, pacing on the patio off the kitchen, intermittently talking on his cell phone and staring hard, out into the still night. I'd assumed he was coordinating our departure with my pilot, bringing Pablo up-to-date on events in Florida, formulating his defense. I really didn't care; my fate had become less interesting to me than my past, all the crossroads I'd come to, other paths I might have taken to avoid coming to this point in my life. When Candace offered her putter-around, Enio leaned into the kitchen and immediately nixed her plan. "If the police find the car before you get it back, then you can be tied to Clint leaving the country."

I had enough sense left in me to be startled that Enio had apparently been paying such close attention to our conversation, but Candace only sighed at the logic. "Well, then, Jack can drop you off."

Enio shook his head. "There will be security tapes." We had been so careful about those during this whole misadventure.

"Well, how will you get to the airport, then?" David asked, exasperated. "*Walk*?"

The Miami-Homestead General Aviation Airport was about only six miles from the Cohen estate, a distance any healthy person could traverse, if push came to shove, without much strain. I wasn't feeling particularly healthy that very early morning.

"He"—Enio gestured toward Jack—"can drive us almost there, and we go now, while we've still got dark. We can walk the rest of the way, maybe a mile."

"No problem," I chirped to Enio, though only for Candace's benefit, to ensure her of how minor an issue the walk would be, the comfort that would envelope me as soon as this last challenge was met.

We didn't dwell on our good-byes. There was no reason to tack an exclamation point onto the end of our heartache—and, anyway, we all understood we weren't really at the end of it. We were only just beginning this new phase of our lives, one to be lived without each other.

Candace hugged me so hard I could barely breathe, and whispered in my ear: "Keep your head up, my dear boy."

David held my hand in his good one for longer than made either of us comfortable, and still neither of us wanted to let go. When he brought my hand toward his face and kissed my fingers—the most natural gesture, and entirely uncustomary —it brought me far too near to our loss. Both of us, I think, were relieved at my deflection: "Jack. Let's head out."

At Enio's direction, Jack let us out of his car on Mowry Street, less than a mile from the Miami-Homestead General Aviation Airport, under cover of a stand of palm trees. There was no light save the still-breaking dawn to illuminate us as we climbed out of the putter-around, and the street was eerily empty. "Call me. When you can," Jack said.

"Get out of here," Enio told him.

Enio and I had jogged for about a quarter mile when Enio dodged into another random stand of palm trees and slowed to a walk, adjusting our pace through the shadows at the perimeters of Homestead for my benefit. I was in good shape, generally, but the day's ordeal had taken its toll and I appreciated the break. "Are we really going to the airport?" I panted as we walked.

"Eventually," Enio replied.

I nodded, impressed that he was not in the least winded.

"I talked with Francisco," he added.

This surprised me. I knew he'd been trying Francisco's cell intermittently, all night long, but I hadn't supposed the effort would be productive. That repeatedly dialing Francisco was on the order of a nervous tick as he figured out our plan.

Enio shrugged. "He killed Henri. The man with the French accent? His options were limited after that. He was going to have to talk to me."

"What did he say?" We walked along for another few hundred yards. I repeated: "What did Francisco say?"

"He's willing to swap."

"Swap what?" I was able to see Enio's face through the darkness, a silhouette against the palm trees and rising sun. "What does he have left to swap?"

Enio turned his face toward me. I saw him grin. "You for Pablo."

I kept apace beside him, my breathing slowing as I recovered it. "Me for— Wait, is someone holding Pablo—hostage?"

Enio laughed. "He promises if I turn you over to him, he will make sure Pablo is in no more danger from his boss."

"Mateo."

"Yes."

"Does he have that kind of power?"

"Of course he does not."

I calculated the mathematics of the situation. "But you've let him think that you believe he does … and I'm your bait."

Enio's face was once again a blank slate. "Francisco is a stupid man. An addict who has run out of drugs, and so very stupid. I think I will keep you safe."

I was not comforted.

Maybe so—maybe Enio could keep me safe.

Or this could be the day I died.

I was shocked to realize that I was too tired, and too sad, to muster the energy to care.

"Have you ever fired a gun?" Enio asked.

I thought about the last time I had done that, at Alvaro's country retreat. How he'd held me at gunpoint until I assured him I would bow to his will and then, as if his threat had been nothing more than a joke between two friends, he'd given me a shooting lesson. "Yes," I said.

"Good." Enio bent and, without breaking our pace, lifted the leg of his jeans and withdrew the Beretta Model 21 Bobcat strapped there. He handed it to me, and I took it.

Chapter 39

THE shit was not good. It burned his nose and left a taste like a household cleaner at the back of his throat.

Francisco could get his hands on any drug the world had to offer but, given his choice of all that was contained in the cornucopia, he'd take cocaine. Generally, he preferred to snort it in powdered form. The high was not as intense, but it lasted longer. It was a good, everyday drug. And, when the quality was as pure and true as what Henri had been sharing—well, then it was as if every day was like a guy was living in a little bit of heaven.

Right now, however, he would have liked to have a rock to light up... light a flame under some badly needed euphoria. Some badly needed confidence. All he'd been able to score—from the dishwasher at the IHOP and for way too much cash—was a tiny, origami packet of powder cut with something harsher than baking soda. Not that Francisco had a problem cutting the product. He was in the business and, among the benefits of cutting in another substance was that it increased your profit. Personally, he liked some inositol powder in his supply—he swore it helped calm his nerves —and maybe a dash of a good pain killer. A little phenacetin. But this shit? He would have preferred laxatives or powdered milk or boric acid up his nose. He suspected the substance he was ingesting was levamisole. It was the most common additive in a batch of coke—almost three-quarters of any coke you'd be likely to get your hands on, on the street, was cut with it. Levamisole was a drug used to get rid of parasitic worms—notably by veterinarians, mostly on large farm animals— without doing too much damage to the host animal, though it was also used in humans as part of chemotherapy for the treatment of colon cancer. Cut with cocaine, it acted as an amphetamine, which made it more desirable in the marketplace but was, right now, making Francisco as jittery as a virgin in a whorehouse.

He wiped a trickle of blood from his right nostril. Shit, he thought as he wiped his hand on the leg of his dark jeans, this shit was bad. What he wouldn't give for one lousy rock, his little glass pipe, and a Bic lighter. The rush would make all of this better. Get his minds off the pythons.

He thought it had been his idea to meet up with Enio in the Everglades. He and Enio and Clint Kennedy and all the snakes. He had in his mind, when he'd made the suggestion, jungle cover. Sliding silently up a river in a— What? A boat. Not a canoe, an airboat—he still couldn't remember if he and Henri had traveled in the Everglades on water—a river, or maybe a canal?—

but he had heard about airboats, and he knew he wanted something with a motor. Not some shitty boat he had to paddle. He thought maybe he was remembering a canal because when he'd looked up "Everglades" on his phone, he'd thought the images of the Buttonwood Canal looked familiar—like boats on rivers in Viet Nam that he'd seen in movies. "Apocalypse Now" maybe. Yeah, he loved that film.

Maybe he was remembering traveling along a canal only because he'd seen actors do it in that movie?

And Henri's hut—was that his imagination too? He turned quickly, hearing laughter behind him, a whole host of people laughing. He spun in a circle, assuring himself that he was alone.

Alone, in spite of the voices that called his name and laughed at him.

And where had he thought he was going to get an airboat—go into marina and hot wire one? He'd abandoned the LeSabre along State Road and done just as Enio had instructed, entering the park a quarter mile south of the Southern Entrance, and hiking half a mile west, into a dry, flat stretch of land, densely forested with pine trees. There was no fucking water to put a boat on. He walked, crunching needles and snails underfoot, batting away mosquitoes and horse flies and spider webs, the fucking birds heralding the rising sun. He wanted to stop and take another hit out of his little origami packet, but the mosquitoes would eat him alive if he stopped swatting at them. He'd probably get more of them up his nose than powder. It was a stupid, shitty idea to meet here.

"Francisco," the voices called, laughing at him.

Chapter 40

I was raw. Feeling raw—tired and stretched to my limit—literally raw. Horse flies made a target of the open wound on my temple, and my wrists, too, where blood had soaked through the bandages Charlotte had wrapped around them. I shook the flies from my hand when I slapped a mosquito dead on my neck. "Why would you have us meet him here, of all places, Enio!"

Enio walked ahead of me, seemingly impervious to the bugs all around him, the bites that were swelling on his face and forearms. "Francisco's idea," he told me. "There was no talking him out of it." He ducked under a branch, calling back, "Watch your head," and adding, "But I think this isn't a bad place to rendezvous—Francisco's an idiot and this place will have him even more off his game."

It was the first time I had heard him openly disparage that man who was supposed to have been his partner in protecting me on my short sojourn to Florida. "Why would Pablo send him up here with you if he's an idiot?" I asked, and then rephrased: "Why would he hire him in the first place?"

Enio grunted. "Because he likes to save people and make them into his sons. Remember Alvaro?"

I watched Enio moving ahead of me, the formidable muscles I could see working hard even through his jacket. "You," I said. "Did you— Did you, you know. Alvaro?"

Enio grunted again. "I had to do something. He was going to get people killed."

Not that I disagreed with Enio, it was just a shock that he'd have taken such an extreme measure. On his own.

"Did you ever tell Pablo?" I asked.

Enio glanced over his shoulder at me. "No. And I would like it if you wouldn't do that either."

I supposed there was a measure of trust Enio was showing in me by divulging this secret. But on the other hand, maybe he just assumed I was going to end up dead by the end of our hike. Maybe he was going to once again ignore Pablo's wishes and just turn me over to Francisco. He hadn't really told me what he planned to do when we found Francisco among all of these pine trees.

I killed another mosquito, this one on the back of my hand.

"Look," Enio said, ducking behind a stand of trees and falling into a crouch. "There," and he pointed.

I squatted beside him and followed his finger. About thirty yards ahead of us, Francisco seemed to be dancing. Some sort of tribal dance that involved marching in place and spinning in circles and slapping his own head. "What the fuck?"

Enio rubbed his shiny head. "Drug addict meets insect infestation." He stood up. "Let's go do this."

"Go do what? I don't know what the fuck we're doing!"

"Follow my lead."

Enio stepped out from behind the pines that shielded us. "Francisco!"

Francisco appeared to spin in a tighter, faster circle in response.

"Francisco!" Enio demanded, and began walking toward him.

Francisco spun again, but this time he caught sight of Enio and stopped cold, fumbling for the gun in his shoulder holster and losing his nervous grip. By the time his wild eyes hit on where it had fallen on the dry forest floor and he had bent to retrieve it, Enio was on top of him, his own gun held in a steady hand.

"I would just leave that right there," Enio said, stepping on the gun, "and back up."

For a moment, Francisco looked as if he might not obey, but then he laughed. "Enio! My friend! Of course, there is no need for guns between us! Where is Mr. Clint Kennedy? You have him with you, yes…?"

Francisco's arms flailed against the onslaught of insects, and he stopped babbling only when his back hit a tree. That was when Enio replied by taking his foot off Francisco's gun and stooping to pick it up, his sight trained on Francisco all the while.

"Pants off," Enio commanded.

"My pants?" Francisco laughed again, slapping at himself. "These *mosquitos* will eat me alive, my friend!"

Enio's back was to me, but I imagined a small smile on his face as he replied, "I would like my friend to please take his pants off now," he said, and I saw him shake the gun in his right hand for emphasis.

"Sure, sure," Francisco agreed quickly. "Sure, whatever you want, Enio." He slipped off his loafers as he unbuckled his belt and unzipped his fly, and then slid his pants down his legs.

I watched all of this with some relief, certainly— Enio had always had a plan, and now he had it under control—but also with some pleasure: Francisco stood before us in his tight black tee-shirt and a pair of red underwear as sleek and tight as a Speedo swimsuit. The thought that he was one of the most beautiful men I had ever seen had not occurred to me before that moment, but it was not merely a passing thought.

I was pulled out of my reverie by Enio shouting, "Socks. Get them off."

It was hard not to laugh as Francisco obeyed, hopping from foot to foot as he shed one sock, and then the other, swatting at the bugs around him, pleading, "They will bite me all over, fucking *moscas*—"

I knew why Enio was having Francisco strip down. He was checking to make sure he had no hidden weapons on him, no small gun strapped to his ankle, no pocket to reach into for a knife. When he was assured that Francisco was unarmed, he called for me.

I stepped out, into Francisco's line of sight. I saw his eyes narrow, but he took into account that he was nearly naked and had a gun on him, and he didn't say a word.

"Clint, what do you want to do with him," Enio asked as I slowly closed the distance between us.

I slapped my face, taking out another mosquito. Tie him to that tree behind him, I thought. Tie his legs so he can't get away. Tie his arms so he can't swat away the bugs. But don't put a bag over his head. Let the mosquitos deposit their itchy venom in his ears. Let the horse flies land on his face and bite his eyeballs. Let the insects feast on him. It was a cruel, satisfying fantasy.

"Clint, tell me, should I kill him here? Or do you want to do it?"

Did I want to do it? Oh, yes. Yes, I did. My fingers twitched on the Beretta in my hand, and I saw Francisco's eyes widen as he followed the motion down my arm. Yeah, motherfucker, I thought, I'm the one with the gun now. I'm the one in control. And I would love to dispense a little justice right here in this quiet forest, on this early morning. All I had to do was to raise my arm.

Aim.

Pull the trigger.

Killing Francisco would feel so very fine...

But for how long?

And could I live with myself after the fine feeling wore off?

I was many things, not all of them in full compliance with existing law, but I almost laughed out loud at the thought of myself as a cold-blooded killer. I thought of Candace, and of David— I thought of my father. Not that I had a hope in hell of seeing either of them in the near future, but if that's what I became—if I impulsively made a cold-blooded killer of myself—would I ever be able to face them again? It would be much better for my self-image if I didn't have to grapple with that sin, and much more in line with my general M. O. to defer. To tell Enio I didn't want to kill him here and now, that I wanted to take him back to Mexico and hand him over to Pablo and let Pablo do with him whatever it was he might want to do. Let someone else do the dirty work.

I watched Francisco squirm, swatting his hands at the flies and squashing mosquitoes when they landed on his arms and thighs, afraid to speak. I relished every swat and squish. Every bit of a fear so real I could smell it.

"Clint?" Enio urged me.

Or, I could just tell Enio no. No, I didn't want to kill him. But he should feel free to go ahead and take care of it. Did it count toward being a cold-blooded killer if you didn't pull the trigger yourself? If all you did was sanction a murder? Exactly how much was the debit in that case?

I slapped the back of my neck, brushed a horse fly the size of a goddamned quarter out of my hair. "We are all being eaten alive out here, Clint," Enio said. "Do you want to put this *cabron* out of his misery... or do you want me to do it?"

Chapter 41

THAT should have been the end of it. When I told Enio that neither one of us were going to put the flailing Francisco out of his misery. Let the poor bastard get dressed, I'd said, and we'll take him back with us and let Pablo decide what to do with him.

Enio had sighed—clearly this was a man who liked decisive action and clean endings—but he tilted his head to me and gave a single nod, indicating he would accede to my wishes. He waved the gun in his right hand toward our prisoner. "Put your clothes on," he ordered.

Francisco—not quite believing his good luck, eyes darting back and forth between Enio and me, still fearful of taking his eyes off either of us —stooped to pick up his pants. He slid in one leg, then the other, and gave a couple of hops as he pulled them over his hips and zipped them up. He left his socks where they lay but, while he wiggled a foot into each loafer, he also wiggled a hand into one of the front pockets of his jeans.

Enio, ever alert, had relaxed his stance while Francisco dressed, but his gun arm was rigid again in a nanosecond— "Hands up! Get your hands up!"

Francisco let out another laugh as he swung his arms over his head, waving what looked to be a wadded-up piece of paper in one of his hands. "Just my candy, man!" he shouted back. "Just my candy, you know? You want some?" He lowered his arms and held them out toward Enio first, and then to me. "I'll share some with you—"

"*Bruto*," I heard Enio mutter, then, more loudly, "Put it up your ass for all I care, but do it while you move— Move!"

"*Movimiento, movimiento*," Francisco sang, nodding his head, shuffling toward Enio, looking at his hands while they opened the cleverly folded piece of paper. He stepped slowly, concentrated as he was on holding that piece of paper with one hand and, with the forefinger of the other, dividing off a portion of the cocaine into a short, fat line as straight as he could manage. He stopped, swatting at the insects that swarmed around the target he made, as he drew even with Enio and lowered his head toward the paper, blocking off one nostril and vacuuming up the powder with the other. He let out a long, throaty growl as the coke hit his membrane, on its way to his blood and his brain, and began walking again only when Enio prodded him with a gun to his lower back. "*Movimiento, movimiento*," Francisco sang again and restarted his shuffle, his focus still on the little packet of paper and dividing out a second line for his other nostril.

Francisco, Enio close behind, had caught up to me when he stopped to suck up the second line. I caught Enio's eye while we waited for Francisco to finish his snort, saw him glare with frustration at the back of Francisco's head, the exact place, I imagine, where he would like to empty one of the guns in his hands.

Francisco let out another jubilant, satiated growl, and when Enio once again prodded him along, said, "*Un momento, amigo*," and plunged the finger he'd been using to divide the coke into lines into the small pile that remained on the paper and then into his mouth, sucking hard, growling. "You sure you don't want some?" he asked, the words rumbling out at the end of his snarl as he turned around, toward Enio, thrusting the packet toward him and—

I wish I had been watching them more closely. I knew as soon as it happened that I would wish for the rest of my life I had been paying attention to what was happening immediately behind me rather than looking ahead, calculating the long hike back to State Road, and the distance from there until we made it to the safety of my plane. How light it would be outside by the time we hit the trafficked road and what a spectacle we'd make in the daylight, trudging toward the airport. How, once Amelie had the plane in the air, I was going to have a shower, and pour myself a whiskey in the biggest glass I could find on board—not in that order—and then pour myself another. How I hoped there was a nice, big roll of gauze in the first aid kit in the galley, the bandages around my wrists were soaked through with blood and filth—

But I wasn't paying attention. I heard Francisco growl again, heard it turn into an extended yowl, a war cry, heard Enio reply with a sound like air being forced through a funnel. Saw the very end of Francisco's nearly perfect round-house kick, his foot connecting with Enio's sternum. Saw Enio fold nearly in two and stagger backwards, the confiscated gun flying from his left hand even as he drew it up to steady his right hand, took aim, got a shot off that went into the treetops. Heard birds scream and scatter overhead. Saw Francisco dive for the dropped gun and spin toward Enio as he was hitting the ground. Saw him fire. Saw Enio's jaw explode.

Felt my right arm raise.

My finger squeezed the trigger of the Beretta Enio had given to me.

Chapter 42

Breathes there the man, with soul so
dead,
Who never to himself hath said,
*   This is my own, my native land!*
Whose heart hath ne'er within him
burn'd,
As home his footsteps he hath turn'd,
*   From wandering on a foreign strand!*

We had to memorize the poem by Sir Walter Scott, Jack and I, when we were in fourth grade. Reciting it was our part in a Veteran's Day pageant our elementary school was putting on that year. For some reason, it was one of the copious bits of memorization from my youth that had stayed with me all my life, and I thought about it now, as Amelie taxied my plane for take-off from the Mérida International Airport. *If such there be, go mark him well...*

I'd returned, just yesterday morning, to Mexico, battered and badly bruised, and made my way directly to Pablo's hacienda, where I found

him much recovered, sitting in a lounge chair by
his pool. He was wearing a pair of white linen
drawstring pants and no shirt, but with a fresh
bandage on his shoulder, and he was smoking a
cigar. "You have come alone," he said in greeting, by way of noting the absence of Enio and
Francisco.

"I have," I replied.

Pablo frowned, then waved his hand at the chair
next to him. "Sit and tell me why."

And so I had. I told him everything. He listened
intently, looking, for the most part, into the deep
blue depths of his pool, sending puffs of smoke to
float over the water.

I spent the rest of that morning sleeping fitfully
in the same small but well-appointed guest room
I'd occupied when I'd last stayed at Pablo's home.
The bed was as comfortable as any I'd ever lain
upon, but my mind was a riot of perilous cliffs
and jagged edges. I didn't wonder that I would suf-
fer with some level of Post-Traumatic Stress Dis-
order after what I'd gone through in the last two
days; I was already presenting with what certainly
seemed like symptoms of it to me.

My cell phone rang while I was tossing around
among the bountiful pillows on the bed; the call
was from David and, of course, I picked up. "Hi,
David."

"Hello, son," he said, a form of address he'd
often used in the past, said now out of habit,
but newly resonating for us both, so neither of
us could speak for a moment. "I wanted to let

you know I've had Jack transfer your funds so, wherever you decide to go, they'll be available to you."

"Thank you, David. And thank Jack for me, too." David made a quick sound—*pfft*—and I continued, grasping, for the first time in our lives, for something to say to him. "And Candace. Please tell her—"

"Yes, yes," David assured me. "She's gone out now for the day. She's stopping by to visit Elmer—I'm sure she'd want you to know that, so you know the man's in good hands..."

"I would never have thought to doubt."

"And then she's going to Jack's boyfriend's... What's his name?"

"Rudy."

"Right. I'd better remember that; I think he's going to be around for a while, God willing. Rudy has a, what do you call it? An atelier, and Candace has ordered some outfits from him and she's gone for a fitting."

"I hear his work is beautiful—"

"Oh, my, yes. Candace says he a goddamned couturier."

"David, no one's asked about me?"

"Not yet."

I allowed myself a moment of relief.

"I expect the police will have a presence at the funeral tomorrow," he added. "Likely to run into Detective Aiello nosing around."

Chester's funeral was what he was talking about. He and Candace, of course, would attend—Chester having been their gardener, and a family friend, for nearly thirty years. Until I got him killed. I had been trying not to think about Chester, because when I did, the enormity of Charlotte's grief, her shaking body and her pitiful cries—and the scope of the strength and sacrifice she had made on my behalf—threatened to overwhelm me. "Will you tell Charlotte..." I began, and then amended my request, "Will you look in on Charlotte from time to time."

"It will be our pleasure."

"Thank you."

"Xavier and I are going to take a meeting with Errol Kushner next week. The judge—you remember him?"

"I do."

"I've asked him to drop by the house on Monday morning. I want to talk to him about what he might suggest as we handle your situation. What actions I might take, and if there's any influence he might be able to make on your behalf, as we clean this up."

I flinched. He sounded so hopeful. As if there was any cleaning up what the cops had on me —and what they would *think* they had on me. Or, maybe, that was just my exhaustion talking. Maybe after a good, long sleep I would feel hopeful again too.

That is, if I could ever actually fall asleep again.

"Don't you think that it's a little... Dangerous?" I asked him. "You know, to talk to a judge about my case. An officer of the court, and all? At least right now?"

David made that *pfft* sound again. Apparently, this was a new habit. "I feel confident in Errol's discretion."

"Huh. I suppose. If you're sure—"

"I once found something the judge lost, Clint. This thing found its way back to me, and I returned it to him. He's very grateful to have it back."

I smiled. I didn't want to know what David was talking about. It was inevitable that I would know eventually, I supposed, but right now it was just another detail to crowd my bruised brain.

"Well, look, I should go now. My physical therapist is due to show up any minute. I need to go spend the next forty-five minutes trying to pick up change and write my name with my bum hand."

My smile grew broader. "Just be patient, David. It'll come back to you."

"From your lips to God's ear," he replied.

"I'll say a prayer."

"Please. If you think that will do any good." I laughed, and David added, "I love you, son."

Just like that. He just came right out with it.

"I love you too," I told him.

Pablo had arranged for us to have lunch together in the smaller, more informal dining room in the hacienda. His chef had prepared a butternut and chayote squash soup with chipotle cream and toasted pumpkin seeds, grilled tilapia with avocado crema, and a small spinach and quinoa salad, accompanied with a viognier from Pablo's own vineyard.

Pablo's maid, Berta, served the first course, the soup, poured the wine, and, with a wave of Pablo's hand, disappeared. "I want to tell you, Clint," he said in between spoonfuls, "Enio and Francisco have been found."

I froze with my spoon halfway to my mouth. "By your men?" I asked. I knew Pablo controlled a landing strip deep in the Everglades, so there was reason to hope, though I knew that Henri had been a primary operative in the area and his death was going to reverberate not just in Mateo's territory but throughout the country's trade. He'd been a valuable player and the lords were going to have to struggle to find anyone half as adept to replace him. Any subject that touched on his loss was a touchy one.

"By a park ranger."

"Oh."

Pablo put down his spoon and picked up his wine glass. Took a healthy drink from it. "There was nothing you could do? Nothing to bring even Enio back with you? I think of you as a son, and you will not go out of your way to bring at least one of your brothers back to me with you? You can do nothing but run to your plane like a little boy to get away?"

I was expecting to be berated for my failure —hell, I had been berating myself for this very thing—but not over butternut and chayote squash soup. "Look at me," I snapped at my host. I spread my arms so he could take in the gash on my temple, the bandages—once again bleeding through —on my wrists. "I'm not one of your goons, Pablo.

I'm not your *fixer*. I'm your business partner. I don't know how to get bodies in and out of foreign countries. Did you want me to carry him on my back down State Road?"

Pablo, to my astonishment, chuckled. "All right, Clint. There is no need to become unhinged."

"Isn't there?" I snapped again. Then I picked up my wine, sat back in my chair and guzzled half of the glass in one gulp. "I need out, Pablo."

"Out of Mexico? Yes, you cannot stay here. Mexico has an extradition treaty with the United States—if the police do come to look for you, they must not find you in this country."

"I mean out of the business. I'm— I'm not built to take this much pressure, and I don't care if you think that makes me sound weak. No one who isn't a sociopath could come out of these last few days unscathed."

Pablo laughed—really belly-laughed this time— and then sat back thoughtfully with his wine in hand. "First, we will get you out of this country. Then, when you are feeling better, we will talk again about your future."

"If I stay in this business, I may not have much of a fucking future to talk about—"

Pablo ignored me. "In the meantime, I will buy your house and your school from you."

I am sure I did a double take.

Pablo shrugged. "Someone must look after them while you're gone. And I need the legacy you promised me, like your school, so why not just take your school? I'll pay what they're worth, and more—and the cash will come in handy in your upcoming travels, you'll admit, yes?" I was still speechless, so he added, "And, if, someday, you find you are able to return to Mérida? Well, then I will sell your house back to you, and for exactly what I am paying you for it. Without a profit for myself. What do you think of that?"

That you are an opportunistic thug, Pablo, I thought, but did not say. That I am being required to leave *my* legacy in the hands of a rapidly fading drug kingpin. That you are taking the only piece of Taavi I have left away from me, and now my love is really and truly dead. "I don't really have a choice, do I?"

"No," Pablo answered, and picked up his soup spoon once more. "You ought to try the soup, Clint. Before it gets cold. It's very good."

I sat in the very back of my plane, a healthy glass of whiskey on the table before me, studying the information on a sheet of paper Pablo had had printed out for me earlier in the day, while Amelie taxied to our place on the runway. It was a list of all of the countries that did not have extradition treaties with the U.S. My choices were limited —they ran the gamut from Afghanistan to Syria —and the only two options that seemed immediately appealing were the Maldives, where I could sweat out my grief in relative privacy on a white sand beach, or Morocco, where I could, conceivably, find plenty of action while blending into the crowd.

Not that there was much urgency about a decision. Not *much.* Amelie had already filed our flight plan and we were headed to Toronto, where we would find relative safety for forty-eight, maybe seventy-two hours, before my name was connected to recent events in Miami and surrounds and good old Lou Aiello started to try to track me down. I had a day or two to figure it out.

The sound of soft static filled the cabin, and Amelie's voice came to me over her radio. "Heard some chatter I thought you'd be interested in."

"What is it?"

"Mateo. He's been assassinated."

I didn't even flinch. I figured that would have to happen. "Thanks, Amelie. Keep your ear to the ground."

"You know I will."

"I do."

I sat back in my seat, watching out the window as the tarmac rolled by outside. Then I looked again at the list on the page in front of me and took a large swallow of my whiskey. And I grinned. I flipped the page over, to the blank back side, reached for the red-ink Waterford pen in the inside pocket of my jacket, and started scribbling:

1. Pablo – king of kings; for how long?

2. Luis – Oaxaca; Pablo's brother-in-law—and heir?

3. Lucas – Veracruz and Puebla; untouchable. Probably.

4. Felipe – Tamaulipas; DEAD.

5. Mateo – Nuevo León, and, briefly, Tamaulipas, and now there are two major border territories without a captain because Mateo's DEAD too...

Get the Water Street Crime Starter Library
FOR FREE

Get four, full-length ebooks—***BLOODY PARADISE***, ***FROM ICE TO ASHES***, ***TROPICAL ICE***, and ***SING FOR THE DEAD***—plus two introductory short stories by the author of ***STAINED FORTUNE***, ***MONEY FAUCET*** and ***HARD CASH*** and lots more exclusive content, all for free!

Building a relationship with our readers is the very best thing about publishing.
We occasionally send newsletters with details on new releases, special offers and other bits of news relating to Water Street Press.

And if you sign up to the mailing list we'll send you all this free stuff:

1. A free ebook edition of the exotic thriller ***BLOODY PARADISE***—"...a spicy thriller..."

2. A free ebook edition of the crime thriller ***FROM ICE TO ASHES***—"designed to shoot the ice down your spine..."

3. A free ebook edition of the eco-thriller ***TROPICAL ICE***—"...well-spun, tautly written..."

4. A free ebook edition of the delightfully noirish mystery ***SING FOR THE DEAD***—Foreword Reviews' Gold Medal winner

5. A free copy of two introductory short stores from the author of **STAINED FORTUNE**, **MONEY FAUCET** and **HARD CASH**—stories from the childhoods of two his most intriguing characters, Alvaro and Pablo.

You can get all this and more,
for free, just by signing up at

**mailchi.mp/waterstreetpressbooks.com/
waterstreetcrimemailinglist**

Did you enjoy this book? You can make a big difference for our amazing Water Street Crime authors.

Reviews are the most powerful tools in our arsenal when it comes getting attention for our books. Much as we'd like to, we don't have the financial muscle of a New York publisher. We can't take out full-page ads in the newspaper or put posters on the subway.

(Not yet, anyway).

But we do have something much more powerful and effective than that, and it's something that those publishers would kill to get their hands on.

A committed and loyal bunch of readers.

Honest reviews of our books help bring them to the attention of other readers.

If you've enjoyed this book we would be very grateful if could spend just five minutes on Amazon or the online vendor of your choice leaving a review (it can be as short as you like).

Thank you very much.

About the Author

JOE Calderwood was born and raised in Homestead, Florida and graduated from college in 1971 with a BBA. For many years he was a practicing CPA in Florida before beginning his career as a serial entrepreneur. He's owned, so far, seven different businesses, currently a fifty-five lot development in Western North Carolina. *Hard Cash* is the third in the Clint Kennedy series. He lives in Western North Carolina with his spouse of six years—though the two have lived together thirty-nine years, only recently the Supreme Court allowed them to marry.

:

The Grand

Enjoy this excerpt from THE GRAND, the first book in the Dean Wister Series by Dennis D. Wilson.

1

SENATOR Thomas McGraw sat back in the hand-distressed, buffalo-hide easy chair and contemplated the room around him. This was his first visit to the brand new, custom-designed mountain home of his lover. When their affair started a little over a year ago, what a sweet and savory surprise it had been to both of them. A business relationship grew into friendship, and then suddenly and unexpectedly exploded into something else—a red-hot, cross-country, obsessive romance fueled by shared erotic tastes. The senator felt sexually liberated under the spell of his exotic lover, and he was pretty sure those feelings were mutual. True, they needed to be discreet for a variety of reasons—indiscretion had nearly cost them everything—but they had worked it out. Although hectic schedules limited their rendezvous to only a couple of weekends a month, the deprivation and anxiety of anticipation made these weekends that much more satisfying. He was generally in a frenzy by the time he could get to her.

The room was the den of a typical ten-thousand-square-foot vacation home of the rich and powerful in Jackson Hole, Wyoming. Decked out in nouveau western, its reclaimed timbers, Wyoming sandstone, and river rock were either complemented by—or detracted from, depending on your esthetic point of view—the original modern paintings depicting bold and most definitely non-earth-toned western landscapes and various forms of neon-colored wildlife. As Tom sipped his twenty-three-year-old Pappy Van Winkle, he studied the visage of a purple and orange moose head sculpted from California mahogany hanging dispiritedly over the fireplace. Damn, any self-respecting Wyoming moose would be embarrassed to know that this is some guy's idea of what a trophy moose should look like. His personal style was more traditional Western—big wooden beams and a glut of real dead animal heads on the walls. But, the sex was still new and novel, unlike anything he had felt before, and he was willing to overlook these stylistic differences for the time being or, who knew, maybe for a long time. As his mentor had told him a long time ago: "Pussy is a powerful motivator."

"I am soooo happy we were able to start our weekend a day early," his lover called from the other room. "I've been so horny this week that I've been bouncing off the walls. I brought back something special for you from Chicago. Just give me another minute, sweetie." Charlotte Kidwell dressed, and undressed, to accentuate her best features: her big green eyes, her long, toned legs, and her perfect bubble butt. Her regular head-to-toe salon appointments, personal trainer, and strict dietary regimen were essentials to the healthy, put-together appearance that women of her age and social status often have, if they have the money and motivation to work at it. In her younger days, her insecure attempts to add sex appeal fell short, and she'd ended up with an oddly unfeminine look with her clumsy and unsuccessful experiments with cosmetics. But middle age had actually softened her features, and as she became more adept at the finer points of female grooming, she began to realize how much she resembled her sister. During what she referred to as "The Sexual Awakening," she had finally developed the confidence in her sexuality to consciously emulate her sister's makeup and dress. Her older sibling had always exuded effortless sexuality, and throughout high school and college had gone through more boys in most years than Charlotte had dated for her entire youth.

The senator had certainly surprised her. Although his belly professed his lust for food and drink and a disinclination for exercise, his face was the opposite, exuding an irresistible cowboy masculinity. At middle age, most people have to choose between a wrinkle-free face and a toned and youthful body. What was it her friend in Chicago called fat? "Nature's botox." He had chosen his beautiful face at the expense of his body, but that was fine with her, because he was a sexual artiste. Certainly no one who knew him could possibly conceive of the hot spring of sexuality that was percolating beneath his surface. In spite of their distinctly different personalities, she considered him her soul mate. The first man in her forty-four years who had ever laid claim to that title. The thought made her giggle.

"Hurry up, baby, and get your pretty little ass out here."

Appearing in the doorway, she framed herself with the hand-on-the-hip pose so popular with women much younger than herself. "You like? I know this little specialty boutique in Chicago, and it ain't Macy's Intimate Apparel."

He liked the look very much. The red lace push-up bra, matching thong panties, silk kimono, and six-inch stilettos appealed to the man who'd had a weakness for strippers in his younger days. Though the untied robe looked more like a cape than boudoir attire, and the entire outfit reminded him of a porn movie he once saw—*Superslut*, a parody of Superwoman, he had to give her an "A" for effort. "Wow, you look like a very sexy Little Red Riding Hood. And where in the world did you find a bra that makes those pretty little A cups of yours look like Cs? Now turn around and let me admire your world-class bootie."

She did a little twirl for him, grinned, and pushed together her bra cups to emphasize her cleavage. "It's called a miracle bra, and see, it does work miracles. Now you just sit there and sip your whiskey. I have another surprise for you." She strutted over to the bookcase, flipped a switch, and AC/DC's "Shook Me All Night Long" filled the room. And she began to dance.

"Oh my." Tom took a big swallow and relished the burn. "You are just full of surprises tonight."

"Just sit back and enjoy, Senator. I've got a few more surprises coming your way."

Watching her rehearsed moves, the familiar hunger began to stir below his opulent belly. And then, in a maneuver that would have been impressive for a woman of any age, she turned away from him, spread her legs, touched her toes, looked straight up at him from her bare inverted V, and twerked. She had been practicing all afternoon, and when she saw the image of her quivering butt in the mirror she couldn't wait to see his reaction.

"Oh, my god, where did you learn that?" The stirring rising now to a different level. And he was also wondering... her dance routine looked really professional.

"I have a very good friend in Chicago who does this for a living, and she's been giving me some lessons."

"Judging from that pose, sweetie, your friend must be an instructor in 'stripper yoga'." The senator, feeling the fire down there, leaned forward and reached for that perfect ass. "Get over here and let me take you the way I like, the way I know you like." Putting his hands on her bare cheeks and grabbing two hands full, he left his chubby fingerprints as indentations on her flesh. Crazed now, pulling off his pants and underwear but not bothering with his shirt and tie, he pulled her thong aside, mounted her, grunting, sighing. Both of them grunting, sighing, grunting some more. And now just the sounds of flesh slapping flesh. And AC/DC, urging them on...

www.ingramcontent.com/pod-product-compliance
Lightning Source LLC
Chambersburg PA
CBHW050355260626
47156CB00003B/734